# The Reinvention of Bessica Lefter

# The Reinvention of Bessica Lefter

KRISTEN TRACY

DELACORTE PRESS

Text copyright © 2011 by Kristen Tracy
Jacket art copyright © 2011 by Ericka O'Rourke

Visit us on the Web! www.randomhouse.com/kids

Educators and librarians, for a variety of teaching tools,
visit us at www.randomhouse.com/teachers

*Library of Congress Cataloging-in-Publication Data*
Tracy, Kristen.
The Reinvention of Bessica Lefter / by Kristen Tracy. — 1st ed.
p. cm.
Summary: Eleven-year-old Bessica's plans to begin North Teton Middle School
as a new person begin to fall apart even before school begins.
ISBN 978-0-385-73688-6 (hc) — ISBN 978-0-385-90634-0 (lib. bdg.) —
ISBN 978-0-375-89738-2 (ebook)
[1. Self-perception—Fiction. 2. Best friends—Fiction. 3. Friendship—Fiction.
4. Middle schools—Fiction. 5. Schools—Fiction. 6. Idaho—Fiction.] I. Title.
PZ7.T68295Re 2011
[Fic]—dc22
2010004844

The text of this book is set in 12.5-point Apollo MT.

Book design by Marci Senders

Printed in the United States of America

10 9 8 7 6 5 4 3 2 1

First Edition

For my mom, Pat Tracy,
who once made me
the fiercest set of bear paws
this world has ever seen.

# ACKNOWLEDGMENTS

Thank you to all my friends and family for your kindness and support: Dad, Julie, Joe (and awesome family), Mom, Doreen Leonard, Ulla Frederiksen, Michelle Willis, Rachel Howard, Cory Grimminck, Amy Stewart, Richard Katrovas, Mark de la Viña, Christopher Benz, Kathie Velazquez, Tracy Roberts, my gardening friends on Alcatraz, and Bunny. I keep getting older and you're still there. Also, there are more of you. It's fantastic. Thanks to Sara Crowe, my agent, for "getting" me and for helping my stories find their way into the world. Both matter. Thank you to the talented team at Delacorte Press who take my doc files and turn them into gorgeous children's books. It's a thrilling process that I tend to appreciate best once it's over. And thank you so much to my amazing editor, Wendy Loggia, who supports, appreciates, and nurtures all my zaniness, bear plots included. How did I get so lucky?

# The Reinvention of Bessica Lefter

# THINGS TO DO BEFORE MIDDLE SCHOOL STARTS

1. Destroy my collaborative diary
2. Get a brand-new look
3. Buy school supplies
4. Hang out with Sylvie
5. Spy on Noll Beck (when possible and convenient)
6. Find Grandma a new boyfriend (preferably one with a boat)

# CHAPTER 1

I stared into the dark, cavernous hole with my best friend, Sylvie. I didn't know what had made the hole or how far down it went or if its bottom contained dangerous sludge. To be honest, neither Sylvie nor I cared that much about holes. The less we knew about this one, the better.

"I'm not sure," Sylvie said.

This was the sort of thing Sylvie Potaski always said. She wasn't the kind of person who would go down in history for leading a revolution where people burned flags or bras. She was the kind of person who would check with other people (several times) about what they thought about burning flags or bras. Some people might consider this a shortcoming. But I didn't mind it. Or that she repeatedly licked her fingers after she peeled an orange. Sylvie Potaski was my best friend.

Sylvie stopped looking into the hole and started looking at our diary again. Every page was full. This wasn't because of me. It was Sylvie. She was detail-oriented. She couldn't just write in the diary that she saw a tree. She'd tell you how green the leaves were and how brown the bark was and how much shade the tree gave and if there happened to be a bird in it. I'd read every word she wrote in our diary. And she'd read every word I wrote. Because our diary was collaborative, which meant that we each paid for half of it and we both got to use it.

Writing in it had been a lot of fun. We'd passed the diary back and forth for three years. At one point, we thought about keeping a blog instead, but then we saw a story on the news about two girls in Utah who had one, and they posted lots of pictures of their cats, and they got over one hundred thousand hits a month. Sylvie and I didn't want one hundred thousand hits a month, so we kept writing in our diary.

Except it wasn't fun anymore. Because I didn't want anybody finding what we'd written. Some of it was stupid. Actually, a ton of it was. And I regretted that. Especially the stuff I wrote in third grade about liking Kettle Harris. He turned out to be such a dork. And if I went to middle school and somebody managed to find written proof that I liked a dork, I'd be bummed for the rest of my life. And ostracized. Which was what popular kids did to dorks and people who liked dorks. It basically meant that you lived inside an imaginary trash can and that nobody talked to you.

Sylvie held our diary over the hole, but she didn't drop it. I hadn't expected this event to take all afternoon. I sighed. I wanted to go to the big irrigation canal across from my house and observe the flotsam, and then go inside and watch television, and then beg my grandmother to drive us to the mall.

"What if I lock it inside something in my bedroom?" Sylvie asked.

"That's a terrible idea," I said. "Anytime you lock something up, you're just begging for it to get stolen." That was why criminals robbed bikes from bike racks. Didn't she know that?

"Sylvie, remember the pages where we left our toe prints and then wrote poems to our toes?"

Sylvie blinked. Sylvie was always blinking.

"And remember all those awful pictures we drew of our classmates with fart bubbles near their butts?"

Sylvie nodded. Those particular drawings occurred in fourth grade. The fart bubbles had been my idea. But she was the one who sketched them.

"The diary needs to disappear. When we show up at North Teton Middle School, we can't be haunted by our pasts. We need to walk down those halls like two brand-new people."

Sylvie looked up at me and did more blinking.

"Just toss it," I said.

She hesitated.

"But what if one day when I'm old, like thirty, I want to look back at how I was feeling and thinking when I was in elementary school?"

"That will never happen," I said. "Trust me."

I wanted the diary out of my life. In addition to its being embarrassing, I thought Sylvie had grown too attached to it. Sylvie held the notebook tightly as she stared down into the hole. The ground where we stood was about to have a storage lot built on top of it for farm equipment. And after that happened, after it was covered with a thick coat of cement, after front-end loaders and tractors and hay balers were parked there, our diary would be buried forever.

"Can I keep one part that means a lot to me?" she asked.

And even though I wanted her to throw the whole thing away, I also had a soft heart. And so I said, "Okay. But it has to be ten pages or less."

Sylvie opened the diary and tugged at a group of pages in its center. After she ripped them out, she folded them carefully and put them in her back pocket.

"What did you save?" I asked.

"My drawings of the ocean," Sylvie said.

And that really surprised me. Because those drawings weren't so hot. When Sylvie finally dropped the diary into the hole, the pages fluttered in the breeze like a bird trying to fly. Except it didn't fly. The diary dropped like a rock. Lower and lower. *Bonk. Bonk. Bonk.* It smacked against the side of the hole as it tumbled. And then the sounds ended.

"Kiss it goodbye," I said. "That thing is in China now."

I walked away from that hole in the ground, feeling like I'd solved something important.

"We're about to have the best year of our lives," I said.

I hurried down the trail, back to the sidewalk. I pulled on Sylvie's hand for her to follow me. Pine trees and sycamores climbed into the sky around us. I stepped out into the sun and took a deep, victorious breath.

"We need to sign up for everything," I said. "Yearbook. Cheerleading. Math Club. Chorus. Book-of-the-Month Club."

"Okay," Sylvie said.

I turned around and grabbed Sylvie by the shoulders. "I feel so happy right now I could sing." But I didn't. I figured I could wait until chorus started. I also wanted to skip. All the way home. But I didn't do that either. Once we got to my front door, I invited Sylvie in for cookies and comic books. And she followed me. Sylvie always followed me.

Then we downed a few macaroons and laughed.

"So you don't miss our diary at all yet?" Sylvie asked.

"No," I said. And I was surprised she even brought it up. Because she still had her ten pages of ocean drawings. Then I pounded a macaroon flat as a pancake and tossed it outside for the birds to eat.

"Getting rid of that thing was the best move we ever made," I said.

And when I said those words, I meant them. Even though they were completely wrong. The rest of that day I felt very good about my life and middle school and my new shoes. Grandma had bought them online, and the UPS man had delivered them yesterday. And they weren't like regular shoes. These had detachable tongues. They were held in place with Velcro. And you could rip them out and put in different ones. You could also go without tongues. But that didn't look so hot. The shoes came with twelve different colored tongues. Grandma said they would match any shirt I owned. She called them fashion forward.

And because I was eleven, and hadn't experienced irreversible tragedy or bone-crushing disappointment, I thought I could graduate from elementary school and start middle school and remain a happy person who enjoyed life.

But that wasn't how things happened. On that fateful day, when I politely asked Sylvie Potaski to dispose of our collaborative diary in a hole, unbeknownst to me, I, Bessica Lefter, had doomed myself. Now all the good things in my life were about to turn bad.

# CHAPTER 2

It was the day after the diary dump, and my mom and grandma and I were shopping for back-to-school supplies.

"I really wish Sylvie were here," I said.

My mother looked over my list and then jerked free an empty cart from a long line of empty carts in front of the store. "Did you know that you need a pocket dictionary?" she asked.

"Oh, I'm very excited about the pocket dictionary," I said. "I'm hoping to find a pink one."

Grandma patted my shoulder. "If you can't find a pink one, you can always decorate it with pink stickers."

"That's a creative idea," I said. Then I smiled an

enormous smile. Because I realized that after shopping for school supplies, I might be able to talk my mom into taking me to Sticker Street, the best sticker store in Idaho!

As soon as we walked into Target, my stomach flipped with excitement. The aisles were packed with back-to-school shoppers. I looked around for people I knew. But I didn't see anybody familiar. I just saw a bunch of kids I didn't recognize with their moms. I followed my mother as she zoomed the cart toward the binder section.

As soon as we turned the corner, I knew I had to call Sylvie. There were two solid rows of binders to choose from. Fat ones. Red ones. Sparkly ones. Tiny ones. Binders with buckles. Binders with straps. Binders with Velcro. Binders with snaps.

"Mom!" I said, pulling her and the cart to a stop. "I need to call Sylvie."

"Why?"

I grabbed her hands. "Because I need to know what kind of two-inch binder she bought so I can buy the same one."

"That's precious," Grandma said.

I glanced at her and realized that she had her phone flipped open and was texting somebody, which meant that I couldn't use it to call Sylvie. Because my mom made Grandma and me share a cell phone. Grandma's thumbs tapped happily across her keypad. I let go of my mother.

"Are you texting Willy again?" I asked. "Doesn't Willy

have a job? Doesn't Willy do anything besides text and be texted?"

Ever since Grandma had joined an online dating service last year and met Willy, she seemed to be in contact with him a hundred times a day. It got on my nerves. Because she turned out to be a huge cell-phone hog. I regretted ever teaching her how to text.

"Leave your grandma alone," my mother said. And then she started walking down the binder aisle again.

"One day I am going to need my own cell phone, and that day might be today," I said.

"I'm almost finished," Grandma said.

I watched her bump into a lady carrying a stack of empty plastic cartons.

"You are not the kind of person who should text and walk," I said.

Grandma snapped her phone shut. "He is so special."

I did not want to hear about how special she found Willy. "I don't know. Don't you watch television? What if Willy is a maniac?"

My mother turned around and wagged her finger at me. "We've met Willy four times. He's not a maniac. You know that."

"Sometimes people hide their maniac side," I said, wagging my finger back at her.

The phone buzzed again. Grandma flipped it open and

smiled. Then she snapped it shut. "I'm ready," she cheered. "Let's shop till we pop."

I was so glad that Willy lived in New Mexico and not Idaho.

"Can I use the phone now?" I asked. Grandma handed it to me and it was still warm from her texting.

"Don't you want to get your own unique binder?" my mom asked. She held up one with a picture of a mare.

"No," I said. "Sylvie and I should match. We enjoy that." Normally, Sylvie matched what I bought. But because Sylvie and her mom had already gone shopping, we had to do it the other way around.

My mother picked up another binder. This one had a unicorn and a rainbow.

"Mom," I said. "Sylvie and I hate unicorns!"

"What about rainbows?" Grandma asked. "Remember, we can cover up anything you don't like with stickers."

I shook my head and dialed Sylvie's number.

"Talk with Sylvie," my mom said. "I'll be in the next aisle selecting pencils and erasers."

She left the cart with me and Grandma, and I waited for Sylvie to answer her phone. Then I got straight to the reason I'd called.

"Sylvie! I'm at Target and there's a mountain of binders and I'm stuck. There's one with a dog that I like. What did you get?"

"I got the two-inch binder with the lighthouse," Sylvie said.

I pawed through a pile at eye level.

"I see one with a fort," I said.

"No. Mine has a lighthouse and a bird and the ocean. There isn't a fort. Not even on the back. I'm looking at it right now."

I couldn't believe it. Had Sylvie bought the last one with a lighthouse? Neither one of us had ever been to a lighthouse. When did she start liking those?

"I don't see it. I think I might get the one with the dog."

"I remember that one," Sylvie said. "It was cute."

I inspected it a little bit more. I feared it was a little *too cute*. My mom came back carrying a large pack of mechanical pencils. And another mom and her daughter rounded the corner behind her.

"Oh my heck!" I whispered into the phone. "You'll never guess who's in the binder aisle with me."

"You sound freaked out. Is it Noll Beck?" Sylvie asked.

That was a good guess. Noll Beck was my neighbor, and even though he was fifteen and I was only eleven, I was madly in love with him.

"No," I said. I whispered so quietly I could hardly hear my own voice. "It's Malory Mahoney the Big Plastic Phony."

Sylvie gasped. "What's she doing?"

"Picking out a binder," I whispered.

"Which one?" Sylvie asked.

"That dog is very cute," my mom said, pointing to the binder I was holding. "Good choice."

I shook my head and set the binder back in the pile of other dog binders. "I'm still shopping," I said.

"What's Malory doing now?" Sylvie asked.

Sylvie and I couldn't stand Malory. Because if you ever did anything wrong, even something small like chewing gum during class, she'd rat on you to the teacher, but then pretend like she hadn't.

I gasped into the phone. "She's got the binder with the lighthouse!"

Sylvie gasped too. "With a bird? And the ocean?"

I nodded.

"What's wrong, Bessica?" my mom asked. "Why are you making that face?"

"Hi, Bessica," Malory said, waving at me.

I dipped my chin down and said breathily into the phone, "Malory is talking to me."

"I know!" Sylvie said. "I can hear her."

"I gotta go," I said. Then I flipped the phone shut and walked up to Malory.

"Cool binder," I said. I pointed to the small bird flying over the water. "I didn't know you liked ducks." Because I knew she didn't like ducks. In fourth grade we'd gone on a field trip to Warm River and she'd sat in duck poop during our picnic lunch and then ended up getting attacked by a duck. It pecked her legs and arms and head.

"It's not a duck. It's a seagull," she said.

"Really?" I asked, trying to plant some doubt.

I could feel my mother standing behind me. "I'm going to go track down your ruler. It says here that one side has to be in centimeters."

I flashed my mom a quick smile. "Cool." Then I turned my attention back to Malory. Her mom was looking at me now. She had thick pink blabber lips just like Malory. And she was chewing gum and tapping her foot like she was in a hurry to be somewhere else. Other shoppers passed by us.

"This is Bessica Lefter," Malory said. "We go to school together."

I waved politely.

"We need to get moving," Malory's mom said.

I was so sad watching Malory hold that binder. But I didn't know what else to say.

"Is that the binder with the lighthouse on it that you were looking for?" Grandma asked. "Where did you find yours?"

Malory pointed to an empty area. I made a very sad face.

"Oh darn," Grandma said. "Maybe we can try another store."

I nodded a very sad nod.

"Were you looking for a binder with a lighthouse on it?" Malory's mom asked.

"Her heart was set on it," Grandma said.

Malory looked very annoyed. But I didn't care.

"Maybe you should give it to Bessica," Malory's mom suggested.

This was a fantastic and surprising suggestion. My mom would never make me give up my favorite binder to somebody I didn't like. Because my mom was loyal.

Malory slowly extended the binder to me and I snatched it right up. "Thank you so much!" And then I left that aisle as quickly as I could and headed toward the rulers and hoped that Grandma was following me.

She was.

"Congratulations," Grandma said.

"Now I need to call Sylvie again," I said, flipping open the phone.

"Is Malory still there?" Sylvie asked.

"We're not in the same aisle anymore. Get this. Her mom made her give me the lighthouse binder."

"No way!"

"Way!"

My mother appeared out of nowhere. "Let's hustle. At this rate we'll be here until tomorrow."

I waved the lighthouse binder in the air. My mother gave

me a thumbs-up sign, which did not thrill me, because we were in public.

"We still need glue and Kleenex and five hundred sheets of lined writing paper and a container of antibacterial wipes."

"What about my heavy-duty scissors?" I asked. Because I remembered those from my list.

"I'm sure we've got a pair at home," my mom said, leading us toward the tissue section.

I froze. "But I'm starting middle school. I can't show up with regular old scissors from home. What if I need to cut something heavy-duty?"

My mom tossed three boxes of tissues into the cart. "Bessica, don't get anxious about your scissors. We'll make sure you've got the kind you need." She looked at me and smiled. "Are you on the phone?"

I'd forgotten that I was talking to Sylvie. "Are you still there?"

"I'm still here," Sylvie said.

"Cool," I said. That was exactly what I wanted to hear.

I felt so happy as I plodded behind my mother, talking to Sylvie, purchasing all my brand-new middle-school gear. I mean, what did I need a red correction pencil for? It was so exciting! Middle school wasn't going to be anything like elementary school. I coasted down the aisles until we'd found every last thing on my list.

Loading it into the car, bag after bag, it looked like so much stuff. I was so excited that it was hard for me to resist hopping. But I did. Because hopping in a parking lot, where the entire city of Rexburg, Idaho, could see me was lame. And after I got in the car, I was very thrilled that I hadn't done anything lame, because three parking spaces away from me, I saw the gorgeous Noll Beck. He was sitting in the driver's seat of his Mustang.

Noll's sunglasses looked so cool that it made me want to buy some. I lowered my head so that he wouldn't see me watching him. I stared at Noll Beck's gorgeous head of dark brown hair as it bobbed to the radio. I wondered what he was listening to. I wondered if he bobbed his head like that when he listened to music in his bedroom or if it was something he only did while sitting in cars. I wondered a lot of things about Noll Beck. But before I could watch him do anything else, my mom drove away and he was gone.

# CHAPTER

**B**efore middle school started, I needed a drastic haircut. Making bangs or getting my ends trimmed wasn't enough. I wanted to become a different-looking person. But I knew my mom might not be so hot on this idea. Because before I did things that were extreme, she always asked me to think about how it would impact me in a week and a month and a year. So I didn't run it by her. I just let her go to work and figured I would tell her when I saw her again, which would be when she got home at three o'clock.

My mom worked five days a week, from nine to three,

for a podiatrist in Sugar City, which is a city so far east that it's barely in Idaho anymore. It's almost in Wyoming. And Montana. And because she dealt with files for people with foot issues (such as bunions and hammertoes) day after day after day, she always thought about how long life was and the consequences of your footwear *and* your decisions. This was not ideal.

Because when you want a drastic haircut, you can't think like that. You have to go to the salon and make your demands quickly and get it over with. So I called Sylvie and asked her to meet me at the mall.

"My mom won't drop me off at the mall anymore because it's 'dangerous.' Remember?" Sylvie said.

"I remember," I said. The last time we'd been dropped off there, I thought it would be fun to buy a Frisbee at the toy store and then walk to the park and play with it and maybe look for boys. And it *was* fun. There were people doing puppet theater. And even though you were supposed to buy a ticket, Sylvie and I sneaked behind the ropes and watched it for free. We laughed our heads off at the emperor and his pet monkey. After the performance, we stood in a line for free ice cream sandwiches. But then Sylvie's mom drove past the park and saw us and demanded that we get into the car, and she made us throw away our ice cream sandwiches. And she gave us a lecture about being irresponsible, and dishonest, and about free-loading.

"Tell your mom that my grandma will take us and that we plan to go to the bookstore and have a nutritious snack afterward," I said. Out of everyone in my family, Mrs. Potaski liked Grandma the most.

"Hold on," Sylvie said.

As I waited, I worried that Mrs. Potaski was going to say no. Sometimes she was a real bummer.

"I have to be home by four o'clock," Sylvie said.

"Awesome!"

I went down into our basement, where Grandma had lived for the last six years. Even though Grandma was old and smelled a little bit like toothpaste, she was still pretty cool.

Grandma sat in front of her computer, pecking at the keys. She was writing an email. Probably to Willy. I launched into my question.

"Grandma, don't you want to do something exciting this afternoon with your favorite granddaughter?"

Grandma turned around and smiled at me. Her brown hair was pulled back into a nice-looking bun. And she was wearing her tangerine-colored lipstick, which meant she already had on enough makeup to leave the house.

"Do you want to water the hedgehog?" she asked.

Because a hedgehog was tearing up the lawn, and

Grandma and I sometimes stuck a garden hose in its hole and tried to water it out of its tunneled maze.

"Better!" I said. "I want to go to the mall!"

"I do need some face cream," she said.

"Cool," I said. But, really, I wished Grandma would stop buying face cream. Even though she only wore it at night, it made her face look light blue and creepy. Like she had demon issues.

When we rolled up to Sylvie's house, she burst down her front steps and ran full speed toward us. She was breathing hard halfway to the mall. Sylvie didn't do a ton of bursting or running full speed.

When Sylvie, Grandma, and I walked into the mall, I was the only one who knew about the extremeness of my plan.

"Should we get pretzels?" Grandma asked. "If you ask politely, they'll double-roll them in the salt at no extra charge."

I shook my head. While Grandma was one of the most nutritious people I knew, her one weak spot was salt.

"You do that," I said. "Sylvie and I are going to the bookstore."

And even though that wasn't the truth, I thought it was pretty close. Because the bookstore was right next to the salon. And Grandma would enjoy browsing the magazines more than standing around a place that smelled like hair spray.

"I'll meet you near the tabloids," Grandma said.

"Cool," I said.

Sylvie and I watched Grandma walk down the mall's crowded corridor.

"I don't like it when you lie," Sylvie said.

I put my arm around her. "I know. I'll work on it."

I was so happy before my world turned to garbage. I remember walking through the mall to the salon, excited about school and my classes and even my stupid locker.

When I walked into the salon, the receptionist didn't even question the fact that I'd shown up without an adult.

"I need a haircut," I said. "Nothing like what I have now. I want something that's full of style." I shook my head back and forth. My dull brown hair slapped my face and stuck to my lips.

"Pebbles can see you now," the receptionist said. "Or you can wait for Duncan."

Duncan had green hair, so I decided to go with Pebbles.

The next thing I knew, I was sitting in a chair looking up at Pebbles's thick, black, freaky eyelashes. Then she tied a smock around my neck and asked me all kinds of questions about my hair regimen. I interrupted her.

"I want a pixie cut."

"A what?" Pebbles asked.

I was afraid this might happen, so I reached into my

pocket and pulled out a page from a magazine. I pointed to the picture of a supercute girl with supershort hair. I'd found the picture in a magazine at the podiatrist's office where my mother worked.

"Where did you get this?" Pebbles asked, flipping it over to look at the pictures on the back.

"A waiting room," I said. "The haircut I want is from Morocco. They're very fashionable there. They still have a king."

"Are you sure this is a girl?" Pebbles asked.

Then I realized that Pebbles was looking at the wrong picture. She was looking at a boy with long hair on top and designs shaved into the sides of his head. "Not him! I want this haircut."

Pebbles gasped. And then she pointed at the correct picture. "But this is so short. And you've got such long and luscious brown hair."

I nodded. I was glad she could appreciate it, even though I thought it was dull and brown. "I'm starting middle school, and I'll be taking six classes, and most likely be a cheerleader, and a member of the chorus, and on yearbook staff, and a ton of other stuff. I need something easy."

"Are you sure?" Pebbles asked. She squinted her overly made-up eyes at me. "Every girl goes through one terrible haircut in her lifetime. Maybe you should think about it and come back in an hour."

I was shocked to hear this.

"Don't give me a terrible haircut. I asked for a pixie!"

Sylvie's eyes were very big. She kept touching her hair over and over. It was a beautiful mop of blondness. *Touch. Touch. Touch.* And I knew exactly what she was thinking. Sylvie Potaski was thinking, *Am I going to end up getting a pixie cut too?*

After Pebbles shampooed my hair, she cut away at it in quick scissor bites. *Snip. Snip. Snip.* My head felt lighter and lighter. Mounds of brown fluff piled up on the floor around me. It looked like somebody had shaved a cat. Then it happened. Pebbles finished and she spun the chair around so I could see myself in the mirror. And I didn't even look like Bessica Lefter anymore.

"Holy cow!" Sylvie said.

"I look awesome!" I said.

"Do you want a pixie too?" the stylist asked Sylvie.

Sylvie looked at me. Then she looked in the mirror. Then she looked at the stylist.

"It feels really great," I said. "I think you'd like it."

"Do you have time?" Sylvie asked Pebbles.

Pebbles looked at her watch and smiled. "I do."

And while I remember thinking that Sylvie looked a

little nervous and abnormally colored, I thought things would work out okay.

Sylvie climbed into the chair and got her own smock tied around her neck.

I was so happy when Sylvie decided to get a pixie! Because it meant that we'd match. And because I didn't have any brothers or sisters, I liked the idea of having one friend who I was very close to in every possible way, even appearance.

While Sylvie got her shampoo, I decided to look at the leave-in conditioner pyramid in the window. That was when I spotted Grandma and she spotted me. She did not look happy. She hurried into the salon.

"Your mother is going to kill me!" she said.

But I knew that my mom wouldn't kill Grandma. My mom loved Grandma so much that she let her live in our basement rent-free and play lame Frank Sinatra CDs over and over.

"She won't kill you," I said.

"Then your father will. Promise me that you'll wear a hat around him."

But I wasn't about to do that. I didn't think my head looked good capped. And I was using my own money to get this pixie cut and I wanted to show it off.

"Where's Sylvie?" Grandma asked.

But I didn't tell her, because I was a little bit afraid to disclose this information. Then we heard Sylvie scream and Grandma raced back to Pebbles's haircutting station.

Sylvie did not look happy.

"My nose looks huge!" Sylvie said.

But I disagreed. "It looks as big as it looked before."

"And my ears look pointy! Like an elf!"

I didn't object. I'd never noticed Sylvie's ears before, but uncovered by hair, they suddenly appeared very triangular. Pebbles tried to fix this by hair spraying the hair around Sylvie's ears so that it would lie flat over her tips. But that didn't look so hot either.

"These sections will grow out quickly," Pebbles said.

I think she said this because Sylvie was crying. I felt terrible. Even though it was sort of unflattering, I didn't want Sylvie to hate her pixie. We were brand-new people now. Didn't she see that? Didn't she want to be brand new?

"School starts in less than two weeks," Sylvie said. "Will it grow out long enough to cover my ears in less than two weeks?"

"Probably not," Pebbles admitted.

That was when Sylvie really started to cry, and Grandma stepped in.

"Your ears look perfectly fine," Grandma said. "And if you want your hair to grow as fast as possible, eat lots of chicken. The protein and the growth hormones will churn out a new head of hair fast."

Sylvie blinked and cried. Blinked and cried. Pebbles reached into her purse and pulled out a compact. Then she showed Sylvie how to apply a line of foundation to her nose to make it look less wide.

"Make sure you blend it in," Pebbles said. She tapped her fingers along the bridge of Sylvie's nose.

"I'll help you do that," I said. But really, I didn't think Sylvie's mom would let her wear makeup. Her mom had told her she had to wait until she was fifteen. And then she could wear lip gloss and blush and that was it.

Grandma bought Sylvie and me each a hair product of our choice. I chose shampoo with sunscreen in it that would protect my hair from harmful UV rays. Sylvie picked a leave-in conditioner that was supposed to optimize strength. In the end, Grandma decided to pay for our haircuts too, which was supernice. Because I had brought money, but I didn't want to spend it.

"I bet strong hair grows faster than weak hair," Sylvie said.

"Totally," I said. And then I nodded enthusiastically. Because a trick Grandma taught me was that enthusiasm always cheered up seriously bummed-out people.

And then, while Grandma dropped Sylvie off at her house, I chose to wait in the car. Because sometimes

Sylvie's mom frightened me a little bit. Because she wasn't a very fun person. In fact, she was a little cold. And stiff. For her job, this was pretty useful. She worked for a local doll maker called Country Buttons. Mrs. Potaski's job at Country Buttons was to paint eyelashes on all the ceramic doll heads. And she never lost control or got shaky, and she sat for hours and painted perfect lash after perfect lash. Which made her a great eyelash painter, but she wasn't always enjoyable to be around.

I watched Grandma lead Sylvie by her elbow to the Potaskis' front door. When Grandma went inside the house with Sylvie, I felt anxious. It never occurred to me that Sylvie wouldn't like her pixie cut. It didn't take long before Grandma was heading back to the car.

"Did you smooth things over?" I asked.

Grandma let out a big, exaggerated sigh. "I'm not a magician." Then she started the car. "Where did you get the idea to whack off all your hair anyway?"

"The podiatrist's office." I was usually pretty honest with Grandma.

"Did you see somebody with a haircut you liked?" Grandma kept her lips pressed tightly together as she drove.

"I saw it in a magazine."

Grandma's eyes got a little big, like she was hearing

surprising news. "I thought they just had foot-disorder magazines there."

"No. I found one with a ton of heads in it. In fact, I almost got the wrong haircut. Pebbles looked at the wrong picture and almost left my hair long in the middle and shaved designs into my sides."

Grandma stopped at a red light and sucked in her cheeks. "Do *not* tell your mother that story."

"Okay."

The whole time Grandma drove home, I kept thinking that she had something else that she wanted to tell me. But she never said anything. So I figured that the pixie cut was going to blow over. Like a storm that settles over your house for an hour and dampens your yard and then drifts away.

When I got home, I went to my room and pulled out a bunch of my new school clothes so I could try them on and admire how they looked with my pixie cut. I also got out all my bags of school supplies so I could hold up various items and see how they looked with my new outfits. I posed with my pencils. I slipped on my backpack. I operated my heavy-duty scissors in front of the mirror. I guess I heard the phone ring. I guess I heard some arguing. But I was involved in a very comprehensive fashion show and I wasn't paying total attention. I didn't suspect that my life was heading toward the gutter until Grandma opened my bedroom door and told me that she had some very bad news.

"Are you experiencing hip pain again?" I asked.

Because when Grandma experienced hip pain, which had happened twice before, I had to sleep in the basement and she got my room. And I didn't enjoy sleeping in the basement, because it didn't have wall-to-wall carpeting or a radio or sunlight. Also, there were big spiders down there.

"Sylvie and her mom are coming by to have a talk with you and your mom."

"But it's not three o'clock. Mom's still at work."

"Your mom is coming home early."

I took a step back. Mom never came home early. Things were more serious than I had realized.

I stood there in my new brown corduroys and pink sweater and sneakers with the pink tongues. "The pixie cut was too extreme, wasn't it?" I asked.

"Bessica," Grandma said. "Life is a fluid thing. It doesn't always go in a straight line. You might want something that is right in front of you, but sometimes you've got to take a journey other than the one you expected to get there."

I wasn't surprised to hear Grandma talking about

journeys, because she was a direct descendent of the pioneers. And so if you let her talk long enough about any subject, eventually you ended up hearing about handcarts, and the whooping cough, and oxen stuck in mud holes. I ran my fingers through my pixie cut.

"Will you be there?" I asked.

She nodded. "I've got some news to deliver as well."

And I wasn't worried when I heard her say that, because I thought I knew what she was talking about. Grandma had been complaining about the air quality in the basement for a while, and I suspected that she was going to buy some sort of air-purifying device. But before she was allowed to buy anything that required electricity, she had to check with my parents. There had been an incident involving an electric blanket, and a massage chair, and a minifridge that knocked out all the power in the house, and in the middle of the night my dad had to do something involving a flashlight and the circuit breakers to get us light again. After that, she'd been put on notice about her wattage consumption.

I changed out of my new clothes and brushed my teeth. That way, if I needed to make a powerful argument, I would have clean and persuasive breath. I remember sitting on my couch thinking that I was going to have an unpleasant conversation. But that was an understatement.

Because until this meeting, I had no idea that Sylvie's mom secretly hated me and had been plotting to destroy my life. I thought she was an okay mom. But I guess that just goes to show you that you don't really know somebody until she comes to your living room and flushes all your dreams down the toilet.

# CHAPTER

"**W**hat were you thinking?" my mother asked me. "And where were you during the big shearing event?" She pointed into the kitchen at Grandma. We were sitting on the couch, waiting for Sylvie and her mom to arrive.

"I was at the bookstore," Grandma said.

"I just wanted a haircut," I mumbled.

Grandma walked into the living room carrying two dishes of fruit salad that she'd just sliced up and topped with crème fraîche. She handed one to me.

"Mrs. Potaski is furious!" my mother said. "She makes me feel like an unfit parent."

Then the doorbell rang. And before I had a chance to tell my mom that she was a totally fit parent, Sylvie and her mom walked into our living room. I took a big bite of my fruit salad. Mrs. Potaski looked like she'd been painting all morning. She had black smears on her jeans and she smelled bitter, like paint thinner. It worried me that her shiny black hair fell onto her shoulders in a very angry way. I looked at Sylvie. She was in the clothes she'd worn to the mall. Her eyes looked red from crying. And that made me feel terrible.

"Care for a dish of fruit?" Grandma asked. "Topped with crème fraîche?"

This was one of the reasons Mrs. Potaski liked Grandma. Because she did grandmotherly things like make dessert. And she didn't produce sugar bombs like other grandmas in the area who made things out of sweetened condensed milk and coconut and butterscotch chips. Her stuff had nutrients in it, even calcium.

"No. Thank you," Mrs. Potaski said. I sat up a little straighter. She'd never passed on one of Grandma's desserts before. I stopped eating. And then Mrs. Potaski didn't even take a seat. She just stood in my living room and started saying horrible things.

"Bessica is a dangerous influence," Mrs. Potaski said.

I waited for Sylvie to leap to my defense, but she didn't. I had to wait for Grandma to do that.

"Let's not overreact," Grandma said. "A bad haircut is temporary."

Sylvie looked so sad. I wished she'd told me that she had such pointy ears. Because we could have told Pebbles to modify Sylvie's pixie cut and leave it longer on the sides.

"I have already had a long talk with Bessica about the haircut debacle," my mother said. "And she's grounded."

This was the first I'd heard of this. I guess my mom wanted to look tough and not unfit in front of Mrs. Potaski.

"That's not enough," Mrs. Potaski said. "I plan to take action."

Action? I had no idea what this meant. Was Mrs. Potaski going to beat me up? Was she going to sue me?

"Sylvie will not be attending North Teton Middle School," Mrs. Potaski said.

This statement was so surprising and terrible that I couldn't even believe it.

"Where is she going to go?" my mother asked.

"I'm sending her to South," Mrs. Potaski said.

"No!" I said. "You can't. Sylvie is my best friend. And she already has her classes. Plus, she's been assigned a locker."

But Mrs. Potaski didn't look like she was going to change her mind. She looked ticked off. "I've called the principal. It's done."

"Over a haircut?" my mother asked.

Mrs. Potaski shook her head. "There is something else."

When I heard this, I held my breath. Because I had no idea what else I'd done.

"Bessica led Sylvie into a dangerous construction area yesterday and instructed her to throw her diary into an open pit."

My mother's mouth dropped open and she looked at me.

"It's gone forever. All her ideas. All her drawings. Every preadolescent musing she's had since third grade. Poof. Erased," Mrs. Potaski said.

"Is that true?" my mother asked.

And I wanted to point out that the drawings weren't so hot and neither were the ideas, but I said something else. "It was a collaborative diary. It was half mine."

My mother covered her mouth.

"Bessica!" Grandma scolded. Then she took away my fruit dish.

"I feel sick to my stomach," Mrs. Potaski said. "I still have my own diary from those years, and I turn to it often as a source of immense pleasure."

"But she kept ten pages," I offered.

Sylvie looked down at the floor.

"Yes. I've seen those pages," Mrs. Potaski said. She folded her arms across her chest and frowned at me.

And I didn't know why Mrs. Potaski sounded so mad. Why would pictures of the ocean upset her?

"Do you know what was written on the back of them?" Mrs. Potaski asked me.

And by the tone in her voice I knew that it wasn't another ocean picture.

"A list," Mrs. Potaski said. And she hissed a little when she said that word.

"Huh," I said. I tried to think of all the lists I'd written in that diary. But there were a lot.

"And do you know what it was a list for?" she asked.

I shook my head.

"It was a list of forty-two regrettable things you did during the fifth grade."

I looked at Sylvie, but she was still looking at the floor. I'd forgotten all about that list. How could she let her mother see that? What was wrong with her?

"Well, we all have those kinds of lists," Grandma said. "But not everyone writes them down."

"I don't have a list like that," Mrs. Potaski said.

And I couldn't take hearing people talk about me and my list like I wasn't even there. "But I did those things a year ago. Plus, I regret them."

"You still did them!" Mrs. Potaski said. "You are a dangerous influence. I only need to look at my daughter's hair to confirm that." Then she looked at Sylvie's hair and groaned.

That was when I realized that Sylvie's mom was most

likely crazy and I became worried that I might never see Sylvie ever again.

Then Mrs. Potaski unleashed a terrible lecture about personal responsibility and key growth years, and I kept wanting to jump in and yell, "I see your point, but Sylvie's my best friend. You can't separate us. That's stupid. And mean." But Mrs. Potaski never even took a breath, and when she was finished she did something that was the meanest thing anybody had ever done to me. She asked Sylvie to say something to me about this decision.

"I think it's a good idea," Sylvie said quietly. "You talk about going to middle school as a brand-new person. This is a way to make sure we're equally brand new."

"What?" I said. I couldn't believe she meant that.

And then I stopped listening to anything anybody had to say. Because I felt that everybody in my living room had become a jerk. Then my mom did a little bit of pleading on my behalf, and even though I wasn't listening anymore, everybody was speaking loudly enough so that I learned even worse news.

"I actually switched Sylvie to South two months ago," Mrs. Potaski said.

This news blew my mind.

"What?" I asked. I jumped to my feet and pointed at Sylvie. "Did you know about this?"

Sylvie shook her elf head. "I just found out today."

I sat back down. But for some reason I kept pointing at Sylvie. Until she started to leave.

"There really isn't anything more to talk about," Mrs. Potaski said. "We should get going."

I watched Sylvie and her mom walk to their car. My mom followed behind them. I thought she'd keep pleading on my behalf. But I didn't hear that. Just silence.

"I know that's not the news you were hoping for," Grandma said.

"I don't even believe that's going to happen," I said.

"Remember what I said about the journey," Grandma said. She tried to hand me back my fruit dish, but I didn't take it. I walked outside because I didn't want to hear anything else that Grandma had to say. Because she was not improving my mood. And then, standing in the driveway, I watched my best friend wave at me as she was driven away.

It was so lame. Even if her haircut made her look a little elfin and bulb-nosed, she still looked like a girl. And the diary was stupid. And I felt bad about those things I did in fifth grade. That was why I said I regretted them. Couldn't anybody else see that? That was when the next rotten thing happened. Except I didn't know it was rotten yet. I just thought it was weird. A giant motor home pulled into our driveway.

"Are you lost?" my mother asked as she walked toward the driver's window.

Then this old guy in a cowboy hat shook his head. "It's me. Willy!"

Why was Willy in my driveway? Why wasn't he in New Mexico, where he belonged?

"Rhoda!" Willy yelled. That was Grandma's name. But nobody called her that; everybody called her Grandma. Except for her Scrabble buddy, Maple, who called her Toots. I watched in horror as Grandma ran to the window and began smooching Willy. I couldn't stop staring.

Finally, my mom exclaimed, "This is a surprise!"

Then Grandma stopped smooching Willy and looked at us. "We're going on a road trip to visit a few places we've both always wanted to see."

And I thought my mom was going to object to this by yelling and maybe even swearing a little, because Willy's motor home was belching black smoke and it was clear to me that this was an unsafe vehicle that my grandmother did not belong inside of. But my mom didn't do that at all.

"Wow," she said. "That sounds like fun. How long will you be gone?"

Instead of letting Grandma answer, stupid Willy answered, "We've decided to take the next six weeks to see some world-renowned caves: Crystal Cave, Jacob's Cave, Talking Rocks Cavern, Bluff Dweller's Cave, and more!"

"Six weeks?" I yelled. "To look at caves?"

"Lower your voice," my mother said.

Just then my dad pulled up. I felt relieved that he was home from work early, because he would talk sense into everybody and force Grandma to continue living in our basement. I loved Grandma. I didn't want her to leave with Willy. It was like she'd gone crazy. Didn't she know that we needed her?

My dad's reaction was not what I'd hoped for.

"Nice to see you again, Willy. Cool Winnebago," he said.

Then Willy offered to give my dad a tour and take him for a ride. Then my mom said that she'd like to check it out too. Then we all climbed in and Willy drove us down the road in his stupid, belching motor home, and I heard Grandma laughing, and Willy laughing. My mom and dad said stupid things like "I've always found caves fascinating" and "The fall is a beautiful time to travel."

And I realized that they were probably sick of having Grandma live in the basement and they were probably going to enjoy having a place to set up their home gym again. It was wrong on so many levels. I closed my eyes and pretended that none of this was happening. I pretended that everything was normal. But as I rode along in the motor home, my world swayed. I had to take a seat at the kitchenette. Silverware jingled in the drawer. Pots and pans clinked in the cupboards. When I opened my eyes, everybody looked so happy. Then Willy pulled into our driveway again and we all crawled out of the motor home.

That was when my father finally noticed that I was a brand-new person.

"Bessica," my father said. "What did you do to your hair?"

And I said the most honest thing ever.

"I think I ruined my life."

# CHAPTER 5

**W**illy kept his motor home parked in our driveway, because he and Grandma still needed a few days to pack and prepare. I didn't even like to go in the living room anymore, because that stupid Winnebago sat right outside in plain view, reminding me that my life was terrible. Stupid Winnebago. I regretted ever teaching Grandma how to go online.

I sat on my bed and tried to think of a way to change the direction of my life. But when that started to seem pretty hopeless, I pulled out a pack of gum.

*Knock. Knock. Knock.*

"Do you need anything from the store?" Grandma asked.

"Willy and I are going to pick up some additional caving equipment."

"Like what?" I asked.

"A medical kit, a couple of headlamp systems, and probably some knee pads."

Suddenly, the thought of a potential injury occurring while they explored caves across America made me think I might be able to reason with Grandma. She opened the door and smiled at me.

"Aren't you worried about your hip?" I tried to make my face look tender and concerned. "How do you expect to examine caves with your current joint issues?"

Grandma sat down on the bed and hugged me. "You haven't brushed your hair today."

I reached up and touched my hair. I could feel my pixie cut sticking up all over the place. But I didn't care.

Grandma ran her fingers through it, trying to smooth it, but that didn't work.

"I don't feel so hot."

Grandma nodded. "Isn't your middle-school orientation tonight?"

Originally, I was going to go to middle-school orientation with Mom and Sylvie and Sylvie's mom. But South had their orientation last night. And since that was the school that Sylvie was going to, and I hadn't heard from her, I assumed that that was the orientation she'd attended.

"Have you called Sylvie yet?" Grandma asked me.

It had been five days since the horrible announcement in my living room.

I shook my head. "It's official. We're on the outs."

Grandma sighed and hugged me again. For some reason, she smelled more like toothpaste now than she ever had before. "Maybe you need to call her and break the ice."

I shook my head again. "What if her mom answers? Mrs. Potaski said some pretty harsh things about my character."

"Don't assume the worst. Do you want to know a secret?"

"Is it about Willy the Maniac?" I asked.

Grandma looked at me sternly. "Willy has been exceptionally kind to you and I expect you to treat him kindly in return. And no, my secret isn't about him."

"Sure," I said. "Tell me your secret." Usually, hearing about secrets made my mind spin with the energy of a thousand monkeys. But not today.

"If you want a certain outcome, you should practice the power of visualization."

"Huh?" I said. Her secret sounded completely bogus.

"Before I met Willy, I used to imagine meeting somebody exactly like him. I pictured us together shopping in a store for caving supplies like knee pads and headlamp systems. I even pictured him pulling into our driveway in a rented motor home nearly identical to the one he has."

My jaw dropped. "The motor home was your idea? And

so was the cave exploring?" I thought Willy had put her up to that. It was part of the reason I thought he was a maniac.

"Focus on the outcome you want, and picture it."

I pictured Willy falling off a cliff and smiled. Then I looked at Grandma and felt guilty, so I mentally put Willy, unharmed, right-side-up on the cliff again.

"Bessica, I want you to have a fabulous time at orientation. I want to hear all about it when you get back."

Then Grandma left before I could ask her to buy me a headlamp system or medical kit or knee pads, because those seemed like cool things to keep in my locker.

After Grandma left my room, I thought about what she said about the power of visualization. I pictured Sylvie in her house standing next to the phone. I pictured myself calling her on my own phone. Then I pictured Sylvie answering. But I got so mad when I pictured this that I started yelling at her in my visualization. Because all she had to do was stick up for me and tell her mom that she wanted to go to North. Not South! North! Then my mom knocked on my door and asked if I was getting ready, and I decided that I would try to visualize this stuff later because I needed to go down into the basement and get some pants out of the dryer.

When I got to the last stair, I saw something that made me very sad. Grandma had gotten out her big duffel bag.

Looking at that thing made me want to visualize something else. I walked to Grandma's bedroom. And I pictured Grandma and Willy breaking up. But then Grandma looked sad and lonely. And it bugged me that Grandma liked dull Willy so much. Because what did he even bring to the table? So I decided to go online and get into Grandma's E-Date Me Today account and learn more about him.

It wasn't hard to figure out her password, because she had written it on a sticky note attached to her computer: *My password is Bronco.* Typing the word *Bronco* and clicking open Grandma's E-Date Me Today account made me excited. Grandma didn't have to be stuck with dull Willy. There were a ton of pictures of single people. And they sounded so much more interesting than Willy. I mean, I found out that he was a retired auto mechanic who enjoyed welding, walking, and salty snacks. He was a terrible fit for Grandma! The last thing she needed was more salty snacks. Why couldn't she see that?

I clicked on the other photos. Edgar in Seattle had been skydiving and was much younger and looked like a lot of fun! Peter in Portland had a face like a movie star and had once played in an orchestra. And I counted at least six retired doctors who owned boats. Why wasn't Grandma dating one of them? We loved going swimming together. It didn't make any sense. I couldn't see any logical reason why she should be dating Willy.

Reading through Grandma's profile, it became clear why she and Willy had ended up with each other. Grandma had filled out her profile all wrong. First, she'd turned her profile to the inactive setting five months ago, which meant that future boyfriends would not be contacting her. So I changed that and made her active. Then, I noticed that she had described herself in a very unflattering way. Where it asked for her body type, instead of selecting *slim* or *athletic*, she'd chosen *carrying a few extra pounds*.

Then I got to a major problem. Grandma's picture wasn't so hot. She was sitting down, so you couldn't even see how tall she was, which was one of her best features. So I looked through our photo files until I found the perfect shot of Grandma. She stood in front of the camera smiling, wearing bright red shorts, stretching her legs. It looked like she was about to run a big race. It must have been before I was born, because I'd never seen those shorts. And I didn't ever remember Grandma running. But the picture was perfect! Because Grandma looked happy and fit and adventurous and fifty.

Then I got to another huge problem. In a section called Tell Us About Yourself in Your Own Words, Grandma had gone on and on about her interests in opera and history and Scrabble and exploring, and it made her sound very dull. So I fixed this by deleting everything and typing: "I am a great cook. And I love water sports!" *Click. Click. Click.*

I knew Grandma might get a little mad at me for doing this. But I also knew that when she ended up with a much-better boyfriend who owned a boat, she would get over it. And probably be very thankful. And eventually invite me waterskiing. Visualization was a lot more effective than I'd realized. Especially when you were as sneaky as I was. When I closed the computer, I hardly felt bad about what I'd done.

"Bessica, are you downstairs?" my mother asked.

"Yes," I said.

"What are you doing? You need to get ready for orientation."

And rather than tell my mother what I was doing, I just decided to get my pants and go upstairs and get ready.

# CHAPTER

One thing I learned about pixie cuts while I was getting ready was that it was really important to smooth your hair when you first woke up. If you didn't do that, and you let it stick up in clumps all day, at the end of the day it took water and mousse and strenuous combing to flatten it down to normal. My mom tried to help me.

"We might need a curling iron," she suggested.

"No way." I had never used one before and I didn't want to start right now.

"It's your cowlick."

"Hit it with more hair spray," I said.

And she did. I wondered if Sylvie had these problems with her pixie cut. I didn't know if the Potaskis even owned hair spray.

After spending twenty minutes making my pixie cut look normal, it was time to leave. That was when I noticed that my dad had a jacket on.

"Let's roll," he said.

"You're coming?" I asked. Because I didn't know dads even wanted to go to middle-school orientations. My dad delivered bread to all the supermarkets and convenience stores and gas stations in the area. He also delivered snack cakes and donuts and buns. After his deliveries he was usually too tired to get involved in extracurricular activities.

"You bet. It will give me a chance to wax nostalgic about my own junior high school days. I sang in the chorus and played the lead in *The Skin of Our Teeth*."

"Doesn't somebody get murdered in that play?" my mom asked.

My father wrinkled his face like he was thinking very hard. "Yeah, you're right. I think it was my child. But I'm sure it was done in service of the theme."

My eyes got big. They would never let kids put on a play in elementary school where a child got murdered, whether it served the theme or not. I started to feel a little bit more excited about middle school, like, even without Sylvie, maybe it had a bunch more exciting stuff to offer than I realized.

When we parked our car at North Teton Middle School, it was already so dark that I couldn't see the lawn. I watched shadowy figures of kids and their parents stream down the main walkway toward the school's entrance.

"This place hasn't changed at all," my dad said. "The flagpole still leans east and the parking lot still has potholes."

Eons and eons ago, before it was called middle school, this was where my dad went to junior high.

"Go bees! Go bees! Go bees," he said.

I looked at my mother like I was going to die.

"Buck, hush," my mother said.

"I don't even think we're still the bees anymore. I think South gets to be the bees and North has to be something else."

"Maybe you'll both get to be the bees," my mom said.

"No way," I said. "We can't both be the bees. So when North plays against South it would be the bees versus the bees? I can't even picture that."

"Me either," my dad said.

As we approached the building, I noticed an official greeter at the front door. She waved to everybody and looked very friendly. But in a fake way.

"Welcome to North Teton Middle School!" the greeter boomed. "Here's a program."

My dad snatched it right away. And when we walked into the school, I didn't even care about the program anymore. Because I was so overwhelmed by how big everything felt.

"The floors are so shiny," I told my mom.

At Sugar City Elementary School, all the hallways and classrooms were carpeted. The glossy look and squeaky sound of the hallways were new to me. And they were lined with lockers. Rows and rows. It made the sound of all the people walking around bounce off them. I glanced at the crowd, but didn't recognize anybody.

"Do you see any of your friends?" my mom asked.

"Sylvie is probably watching TV," I said.

My dad saw somebody he knew and waved happily. "Hi, Lowell!" He looked at me and grinned. "Back in the day, we sang in chorus together. I think he teaches here now."

I looked at Lowell and then looked away. I didn't know what he taught, but I didn't want him as a teacher. I wanted to be brand new, and that meant getting teachers nobody in my life knew or had had before.

In front of the doors to the gymnasium, there was a long table. It was for picking up your class schedules. I knew what classes I'd registered for, but I didn't know what order I was taking them in. I felt so anxious as my mom told the person working behind the table my name. "Bessica Lefter."

"PE last. PE last," I chanted. Because if I had to sweat, I wanted to do that right as school was ending, not at the beginning of my day.

My mom took the papers and gave them to me. "Don't lose them."

"Duh," I said.

"What?" my mom asked.

Then I realized that saying *duh* probably sounded rude and so I said, "Okay."

We walked into the gymnasium and it smelled like pine trees and chemicals. The floor shined worse in there than it did in the hallways. I felt like I needed sunglasses. I mean, I could see my reflection.

"I played basketball on this court," my dad said.

I watched in horror as my dad dribbled an imaginary ball and shot it at the folded-up basketball hoops. I clutched my schedule closer to me.

"Can you tell Dad to please chill out?" I asked.

"Buck," my mother said. "Let's find some seats."

My dad moved in a bouncy and excited way. "Let's go up." He climbed the gymnasium stairs two at a time.

"I usually like sitting closer to the floor," I mumbled.

"Is this good?" my dad asked.

He was on the row farthest away from anything.

"Is that okay?" my mom asked me.

"Will I be able to hear anything?"

"You'll be able to hear everything!" my father boomed. "The acoustics are great in this place."

It was almost like my dad thought that *he* was going to start middle school. Which he clearly wasn't. Because he was over forty and worked full-time. If Sylvie had been there with me, watching him act this way, we could have laughed a little. But watching my dad act hyper, without Sylvie, didn't make me want to laugh at all.

"After the orientation we'll go find your locker and stop by all your classrooms so you know where they are," my mom said.

I noticed my dad waving to somebody else. "Mom," I whined. "Make Dad stop doing that."

"He's just being friendly."

"It's killing me," I said. Because it was.

"It's your dad's friend, Mr. Bradshaw. They work together. He just got divorced. Be nice."

I got a little excited. "He should try out E-Date Me Today. There are a lot of single people on that website. Some of them own boats and are very good-looking."

"Do not bring up dating websites," my mother said. She wrinkled her forehead at me in a grumpy way.

Then Mr. Bradshaw came over and sat next to us. And he brought his son. And I couldn't even tell whether or not that kid was cute, because he wouldn't look at me.

"Bessica, this is my friend Mr. Bradshaw and his son, Blake."

I waved. But he still didn't look at me. Then my mom started pointing to different rows.

"Do you see anybody you know?" she asked.

I looked behind me. I looked to my left. And right. Then I peered down at the heads in front of me.

"Mr. Bradshaw and Blake," I said.

"You know what I mean, Bessica."

I looked around the gymnasium. I knew that my mom was worried about the same thing that I was worried about. Without Sylvie, I wasn't going to know many people. When most people start middle school, they do it with their friends from grade school. But that wasn't going to happen to me. Because the middle school got too crowded, and until they could build a new school, they decided to split the sessions. And so all the kids who went to elementary schools in the north part of the county—Flat Creek, Snake River, and Buffalo Valley—got assigned to early-day sessions at North Teton Middle School, and all the kids who lived in the south part of the county—Powderhorn, Teton Village, and Sugar City—got assigned late-day sessions at South.

Sylvie and I lived so close to the border that we got to choose, and I chose North and so did she. Even though we wouldn't know anyone from Flat Creek or Snake River or Buffalo Valley. Because we wanted to be brand new. Now I wasn't going to know anybody.

"You'll know somebody from dance class," my mother said.

"Dance class?" I asked. "You mean the tap clinic Sylvie and I took last spring? The only person I talked to in that class was Sylvie. And the teacher, Mrs. Chico. Is Mrs. Chico here?" I glanced around.

"You'll know people from your book group at the library," she said.

I tried to remember who was in that group. I clearly remembered Sylvie and the librarian, Ms. Grimminck, but I couldn't really picture the other people. We read a lot of Roald Dahl and Sharon Creech. And there were pretty good snacks.

"Wasn't she in your library group?" my mom asked.

I followed her finger to an oily-headed girl in the front row.

"Maybe," I said. "But I think she had an odor issue."

"Oh," my mom said sympathetically. "Don't worry. You'll make friends."

I looked from face to face. Sitting in this huge clump of people, making friends seemed fairly impossible.

"You're not the bees anymore," my father said, pointing to the paper he was reading. "You're going to be assigned a new mascot. There's going to be a vote."

"Oh," I said. I didn't really care too much about mascots.

"Either the grizzly bear or the gray wolf," my dad said. "Pretty cool choices."

I started reading my schedule. Finally, good news. "I got PE last. And first period is nutrition!" I was excited to learn this.

"Good," my mom said. "I think they're starting."

We all watched as a short woman walked out into the center of the gymnasium and stood behind a microphone.

"Welcome to middle school! I'm Principal Tidge."

Everybody clapped. But I didn't, because I didn't want to drop my schedule.

"We have an exciting year in store for you. Let's take a minute to go over some important rules."

And then Principal Tidge went on and on about all the stuff we weren't allowed to do in middle school. For instance, we couldn't bring any electronic devices to school. And we weren't allowed to use cell phones on school buses, except for athletic travel. And we couldn't wear our backpacks in the hallways, because they were bumping hazards. We had to keep them in our lockers or cubbies. And if we damaged our lockers or cubbies, we would be fined.

And if we missed a class, we had to get our teachers to sign approved absentee slips the day we returned. And then Principal Tidge listed everything that was considered a weapon, which we were not allowed to bring to school. It was a long list.

"No guns, knives, laser pens, bats, metal pipes, chains, throwing stars, chemicals, nunchaku, knuckle-dusters, crossbows, explosives, razors, muffling or silencing devices, fireworks, or any replica weapons."

"I've never even heard of nunchaku or knuckle-dusters," I whispered to my mom.

"That's a good thing," my mom said.

There were a bunch of other rules too. About fighting and tobacco and truancy and public displays of affection. For some reason, during that part of the lecture, I glanced at Blake. And he did not return my glance.

"They run a tight ship," my dad said.

"They have to," Mr. Bradshaw said. "These days, kids are crazy."

I leaned closer to my mom. "We are not crazy," I whispered.

"They're just talking," my mother said.

After about a trillion minutes of lecturing, Principal Tidge finally got to the end. "As for our school colors, before the split we were green and gold. We gave the color green to South."

The audience broke into boos. But I wasn't totally sure why. I always thought green was a pretty lame color.

"But we kept the gold and we've added purple. So they are your new school colors. Purple and gold!"

We all cheered at this, because apparently we were all huge fans of purple and gold.

"And as you might have read in the handout, we're still finalizing our mascot. We're deciding between the grizzly bear and the gray wolf. The second week of school we plan on holding a class vote!"

Then I heard a very embarrassing sound. My dad and Mr. Bradshaw were chanting, "Wolf, wolf, wolf." And then, as if my reputation didn't matter at all, Mr. Bradshaw howled like a wolf.

Blake scooted down the bench, away from his dad. I could relate. I wished Blake had sat by me, because maybe we would have hit it off.

As the people started to file out, my dad stayed to talk to Mr. Bradshaw.

"Bye, Blake," I said. "I'm going to go find my locker and my classrooms."

Blake shrugged at me.

I said to my mom as we climbed down the stairs, "Blake isn't very friendly."

"He's a boy. At this age they often act like clams."

We found my locker right away.

"It's in a good spot," my mom said. "Right by the stairs."

I had no idea why that made it a good spot.

"I wonder where Sylvie's locker is," I said. I sort of wanted to see it. If we ever made up, which seemed doubtful, I thought maybe I would leave a sticker on it. For her birthday.

"Do you remember her number?" my mom asked.

I shook my head. I felt terrible, because even though Sylvie had told me her number, I'd forgotten it.

My mom and I wandered the halls until we found all six of my classrooms. Lots of people were doing the same thing. If I'd gone to elementary school with them, I'd have known which kids were the ones I wanted to be friends with and I could have struck up conversations with them. But I didn't. So I spent a lot of time judging them by their shoes. I figured anybody wearing superwhite sneakers was a dork. And anybody wearing smelly old sneakers was a dweeb. My shoe-based potential friendship–evaluation process got trickier when kids wore shoes that weren't sneakers.

Lots of girls were wearing shoes that looked like ballet slippers. They looked pretty and comfortable.

"I like those shoes," I told my mom. "They might be made out of velvet!"

My mom lowered my schedule and looked at the wrong shoes. I pointed my finger in the direction of the correct shoes as they walked out the door. "There! There!" I said.

"Do you want to ask her where she got them?"

"No," I said. Because that girl was basically gone. Then I looked at my shoes and realized that they had grass stains on them. I hoped that nobody had noticed and judged me. We walked out of the classroom.

"This way," my mom said, pointing down the hallway to the stairs. I followed her all the way to the gym. "Well, those were all your classrooms."

But there was a problem. I had already forgotten where they were.

"This place is a maze," I said.

"You'll learn it," my mom said.

"I don't know," I said. I watched other kids talking in groups by their lockers. I wondered how long it would take me to meet people I wanted to talk to by my locker. I wondered what kind of person would have the locker next to mine.

After we rounded a corner, we ran into my dad, staring into the trophy case. Inside it they had pictures of all the sports teams from every year since the school was built. They also had group pictures of the cheerleaders. They looked so happy. I stared at their glossy smiles. I wondered if I would be as happy in middle school as they were.

"It feels like it was just yesterday that I was a seventh grader strutting down these halls," he said.

I looked back at the trophy case and then at my dad. "Well," I said, "it's been a lot longer than that."

# CHAPTER

## 7

I really wanted to call Sylvie. But more than that, I wanted Sylvie to call me and apologize for switching schools and abandoning me and letting her mom read my list of fifth-grade regrets. And then I wanted her to switch back schools. But she never did that. It made my life feel pretty empty. And it was only getting emptier.

I sat on Grandma's bed while she packed for her trip with Willy. I hadn't even seen her check her email in days. Which meant that she didn't know about all of her potential boyfriends on her now-active E-Date Me Today account. It was a big bummer. I should have tried to wreck her relationship with Willy, the maniac welder, a long time ago. Because now she was really leaving and there was nothing I could do. I felt like I wanted to puke, and I never wanted to do that, even when I had the stomach flu.

"You look so sad," Grandma said.

I watched her fold her bathing suit and put it inside her giant duffel bag.

"I am so sad," I said.

"Have you given up on your visualization exercises?" Grandma asked.

I nodded. "Pretty much."

"That's too bad."

"Whatever," I said.

"Don't be a moper. Stay positive."

"I will never be friends with Sylvie again because Mrs. Potaski positively hates me."

"Mrs. Potaski doesn't hate you," Grandma said.

I slapped the bed. "Of course she does. She thinks I'm a bad influence. I'm not a bad influence. I'm just excited about life and so I seek out interesting things to do."

Grandma packed a stack of bras and looked at me with a lot of concern. "I'm going to tell you something my grandma once told me."

And I braced myself, because Grandma Lefter's grandma had been raised on a farm and so her advice usually had something to do with cow herding or weasel removal.

"If a bull is chasing you through a field, it doesn't do

you much good to ask yourself, 'What does this bull have against me?'" Grandma patted my knee lovingly and resumed packing. "Just step aside until the bull forgets about you."

"I detest bulls," I said.

"And maybe the bull resents that," Grandma said.

This advice seemed pretty unhelpful. Grandma smiled at me, but I didn't smile back.

"My life sucks."

I tried not to watch Grandma pack her underwear. She was taking a lot. "Bessica, your life doesn't suck. Everybody has jitters before the first day of school."

"Jitters?" And that's when I realized that Grandma was so busy thinking about her upcoming trip with Willy that she had overlooked the magnitude of my situation.

"I'm not going to know anybody," I said. "Don't you remember? Teton Middle School got too crowded and so they decided to split the sessions into North and South. North is early-day and South is late-day. Sylvie and I lived so close to the border that we got to choose, and I chose North and so did she. When I start middle school I will know zero people." I held up both of my hands and bent my fingers to make a circle. "Zero."

"Some people consider zero to be a good starting point."

Then I started getting very frustrated, because my own

grandma didn't understand how horrible my life had become.

"I won't know the dorks from the dweebs. In fact, I might be mistaken for a dork or a dweeb. I don't even know what these people wear! For all I know they might dress in beaver pelts."

"Calm down," Grandma Lefter said. "Other than actual beavers, you won't encounter anyone clad in a beaver pelt. It's not that dramatic."

But this only made me talk louder.

"I am going to get shoved into a trash can. Or somebody is going to challenge me to a fight on the T."

"It's been my experience that only underweight boys get shoved into trash cans, because it's a very gender-specific form of hazing. And what's the T?"

"It's this concrete area in front of the school that's shaped like the letter *T*. And it's where seventh and eighth graders lure unsuspecting sixth graders so they can smack them around and knock them out."

"Bessica, is that true?"

"It's totally true! That's why I'm mentioning it."

"Well, if somebody challenges you to a fight on the T, I want you to run and get a teacher as fast as you can."

This wasn't what I wanted to hear at all. Then my mom called down the stairs.

"Willy is here," my mom said.

Willy walked into Grandma's room wearing a belt buckle the size of a hubcap. And then he gave her a quick smooch and I felt myself gag a little.

"I'm almost done," she said.

"I think I'm going to make myself a cup of tea," Willy said.

"Good idea," I said. Because he was ruining my conversation with Grandma. And also my life.

Then she looked at me with a very serious expression and zipped up her duffel.

"Bessica Lefter, I want you to remember who you are and where you came from," Grandma said.

"I know. I know," I said. "The pioneers."

"No, I'm talking about your name." She smiled at me in a very forced manner. "Do you know who chose your name?"

"Grandpa Lefter," I said. I'd heard this story before. But I didn't interrupt her.

"He wanted you to be named after a gifted and original woman. Dr. Bessica Raiche built an airplane out of bamboo and silk in her living room. She used bicycle wheels and a marine motor to make the propeller. And in 1910 she became the first American woman to intentionally pilot a solo flight. She had a mind ahead of her time."

And I didn't bother bringing up the fact that Dr. Bessica Raiche had crashed the plane later that day.

"You are very special," Grandma Lefter said. "And I have no doubt that when you show up at North Teton Middle School, you will win friends left and right."

I could feel my throat tighten. I wanted to believe what she was saying.

Then I heard Willy coming down the stairs again. And I looked at Grandma and asked a very serious question. "Don't you wish that Willy had a boat?"

She smiled. "Boats are nice, but I like Willy just the way he is."

I raised my eyebrows. "So you do wish that he had a boat?"

And then boatless Willy the Maniac Welder walked into Grandma's room and I couldn't stand looking at him, so I left.

# CHAPTER

The motor home was packed and I stood on my lawn ready to die. Grandma had her arm around me, but I just kept glaring at Willy.

"When will you be back?" I asked even though I already knew. I figured making her admit to staying away for that long would make her feel tremendously guilty.

"Six weeks," Grandma said, hugging me to her side.

She kissed the top of my head and then hugged my mom and dad. And then Willy tried to hug me, but I put my hands up and gave him a stop sign. "I only hug my family members."

"Bessica," Grandma scolded.

"I am very upset. I am not in the mood to hug strangers."

My mom came and stood next to me. "Willy isn't a stranger."

I clucked my tongue. It was almost like Willy had brainwashed her.

And then it happened. Grandma got into the motor home and waved to me and Willy got into the motor home and waved to me, and they pulled out of the driveway. I'd thought I hated looking at the motor home parked in my driveway. But I hated watching that motor home pull out of my driveway a whole lot more.

"I'll miss you, Bessica!" Grandma called from her window as they rattled down the road.

"Wow," Dad said. "I bet they have the time of their lives."

And I thought that was a pretty stupid thing to say. Because there was no way that Grandma was going to have the time of her life with Willy.

"Maybe you should call Sylvie," my mom said.

I shook my head. "We're not talking."

"Don't you think it's time that you made up?"

I rolled my eyes. My mom was so naïve. Did she think that all it took to make up was a phone call? Because I didn't think that.

Then I sat down in the grass and started ripping it out.

"Bessica, tearing apart the lawn is not a solution to your problems," my mom said.

"Actually, if you want to move over by the sidewalk you could pull out some of the crabgrass," my dad said.

"Bleh!" I said. Then I fell back into the grass and stared directly at the sun and waited to go blind.

"Come inside," my mom said. "We've got a surprise for you."

I closed my eyes, but I could still see the sun. "Every surprise I've gotten this month has been terrible."

"You'll like this one. A lot!" my mom said.

When I opened my eyes, my mom had her hand out to help me up and my dad was in the garage digging through his tools. I trudged back to the house and sat at the kitchen table and waited for my surprise.

"Is it a dog?" I asked. Because I thought that might actually make me feel better.

"No. When did you start wanting a dog?" my mother asked.

I shrugged. "Five minutes ago."

My mother set a wrapped package on the table. I picked it up and tore off the paper.

"It's a cell phone!" my mom cheered.

Looking at my brand-new cell phone bummed me out. Because if I'd gotten it at the beginning of summer, I would have had people to call, like Sylvie. But getting it now just reminded me that I didn't have any friends and that Grandma had abandoned me.

"Since Grandma took the cell phone, I figured you'd need your own."

I lifted up the box and turned it over. I guess it looked cool. But it was hard to feel excited.

"Who are you going to call first?" my mom asked.

I could feel my eyes getting a little watery. And I think my mom noticed this.

"I know. I know. Let's charge it up and then you can call me," she said.

"But we're talking right now."

"It will give you a chance to use it," she said.

Then my dad came inside. "Trimmed the crabgrass." Then he glanced at me and my phone. "Neat!"

"Yeah."

"Who are you going to call first?" my dad asked.

"Mom," I said. Then I held back a sniffle.

Mom and Dad looked at each other and then Mom came and sat down next to me, and Dad went back to the garage.

"I have another surprise for you," she said.

"Is Sylvie coming to North?" I asked.

She shook her head.

"Have you switched me to South?"

"Honey, as soon as I found out about Sylvie's switch, I called the school, but they said it was impossible to make any changes."

"Impossible," I mumbled.

"I know you're worried about making friends on Monday, so I set up a lunch date for you tomorrow."

I looked up in panic. "Is it with the odor girl from the library?"

"Labels are mean. Stop that. No. I didn't invite your library friend."

"Is Mrs. Chico coming?" I joked.

"No."

I got very delusional and excited. "Sylvie?" I asked. "Sylvie is coming over for lunch?"

My mother shook her head. "I was trying to let you iron that one out. Do you want my help?"

"No," I said, putting my head down next to the table's overflowing fruit bowl. "Just tell me who I have to eat lunch with."

My mother smiled. "Marci and Vicki Docker."

"Who?" I had never heard of these people.

"The Docker twins."

I pulled a green grape from the bowl and rolled it around under my pointer finger. "How do you know them?"

"Marci got a stress fracture in her foot. She's a cheerleader. We fitted her for orthotics. She's delightful! She and her sister Vicki go to your middle school. Vicki is the mascot."

"They let a girl be the mascot?"

"It's the twenty-first century, Bessica. Girls can be anything they want to be."

"I know that. But didn't Dad say that the new mascot was going to be a bear or a wolf? Those seem like boy beasts."

"Vicki was a bee."

I guess it couldn't hurt to know a cheerleader and a mascot. But, even though we were fighting and no longer on speaking terms, I would have preferred to be eating pizza with Sylvie. I let out a big sigh of disappointment.

"I can't believe you're not more excited about this. I'll make you a pizza. It'll be like a party!"

I tried not to gag when my mom said this, because it was pretty obvious to me that it was not going to be like a party at all.

"Why aren't you smiling? In two days you're going to be in middle school. Aren't you curious about what to expect?" My mother was trying too hard. Her excitement didn't sound genuine. It sounded desperate.

"I expect to feel sad and lonely and terrible and come home with a mountain of homework strapped to my back."

"I think talking to Marci and Vicki will alleviate a lot of this emotional baggage."

"Whatever," I said. Then I stood up and walked to the basement stairs.

"Where are you going?" my mom asked.

"To Grandma's room so I can be stabbed by her absence a little bit more," I said.

And my mom didn't object to this. When I got to Grandma's room, it felt so empty. She'd taken all the sheets off her bed and some of her drawers were completely cleaned out. She'd even taken her slippers. I sat at her desk and stared at her computer. Then I turned it on and logged into her E-Date Me Today account. I couldn't believe it! There were over fifty emails in her inbox.

It was such a bummer that she was on the road. I wanted to open up the emails and read them and maybe write back to all the men who owned boats. But that felt wrong. Because changing Grandma's account to find a new boyfriend felt like it was only a little wrong. Sending messages to these potential boyfriends and pretending to *be* Grandma would almost feel like a crime.

I turned off the computer and crawled onto her bed. Then I stared at the emptiness again. The closet. The drawers. She'd even taken down her terrible movie picture of Ace Drummond in *Squadron of Doom*, leaving her big white wall blanker than blank. That was when it hit me that I could not live with things the way they were. I needed Willy out of the picture. So I turned on Grandma's computer and went back into her E-Date Me Today account.

I started to click the messages open. The men who sent

pictures all looked great! Some of them wore cowboy hats. Some of them wore baseball caps. And some of them were bald, so I deleted those. Willy had hair and I felt like I had to replace him with another guy with hair. It didn't take me long before I spotted some good ones. Gary in Montana owned a ranch. Jim in Utah was a retired fireman. This was fantastic news. Because I knew that Grandma would love to date a hero!

So even though it was the wrong thing to do, I decided to write to some of these potential boyfriends so they wouldn't lose interest. I tried to make Grandma sound as interesting and single as possible.

> **Hi, Jim! Thanks for writing. I'm off exploring caves at the moment, but will be back soon. I would love to learn more about you. Please send more pictures. When I get back, maybe we can get sandwiches.**

I didn't have all the time in the world. So I only responded to twenty-seven emails. And I didn't always suggest getting sandwiches. Sometimes I suggested getting together for pie. When I was finished I went upstairs and curled up on my own bed.

Then I flipped open my phone. A cartoon polar bear danced on a small chunk of ice. I'd solved one problem in my life, but I still had others. I closed my phone. Then I opened it again. Right at that moment, I wanted to call Sylvie more than I'd ever wanted to do anything. I dialed her phone number digit by digit. But instead of pressing the Send button, I pressed Cancel. I felt tears slip out of my eyes. My throat had a lump in it so big that it felt like it had closed off my throat.

Even though I wanted to call Sylvie, there was no way I would ever do that. Because she hurt me so much when she said she wanted to go to South and be brand new without me. She hurt me worse than anybody had ever hurt me in my life. And I wanted her to try to fix it. I wanted *her* to reach out to *me*. And if that meant waiting for a couple of weeks, I was willing to wait.

Tears kept slipping down my face. And even though I shouldn't have wished for this, I secretly hoped that Sylvie felt this way too. I hoped she was sad and miserable and lonely and crying on a bed in her house. I hoped that by not calling her, I was hurting her as much as she'd hurt me.

# CHAPTER

**B**efore the Docker twins arrived, I decided to play with my hair and also pick out a brand-new outfit to wear. I wanted to test-run some of my wardrobe. I picked a lavender shirt with glitter around the collar, and a pair of jeans. I also put on my new shoes and selected the detachable lavender tongues. When I came out to the kitchen for lunch, my mother looked thrilled.

"You look fantastic! And I like your school spirit!"

I looked down at myself. I didn't know what about me suggested school spirit.

"All that purple!" my mother said.

"This is lavender," I corrected her.

Then my mom winked at me and the doorbell rang and I sat down and prepared to meet the twins. When they rounded the corner into my kitchen, it was just like I expected. I felt like I was meeting the same person twice, except one of them was wearing a bunch of bracelets.

"I'm Marci," the first one said. She lifted up her hand and waved, her bracelets jingling around her arm.

"I'm Vicki," the second one said in the exact same voice. She did not wave. They both had matching brown bobs with bangs and pink lipstick, and they wore shorts that showed off their long tan legs. Just by the way they entered my kitchen, I could tell they were popular.

"I'm Bessica," I said. "My mom made this pizza."

Then I pointed to the pepperoni pizza on the table. Both Marci and Vicki sat right down.

"Are you nervous?" Marci asked.

I didn't really think that was a good opening question. "I'm okay," I said.

"Oh," Marci cooed. "You sound nervous. You shouldn't be. We're going to tell you the inside scoop about everything."

"Totally," Vicki said.

"Great!" my mom said. She put a pile of napkins down on the table and then gestured to the window. "I'll be outside doing yard work. Yell if you need anything."

When the back door slammed shut, Marci's eyes lit up and she grabbed the pizza slice with the most pepperoni on it.

"We'll tell you all the stuff you need to know," Vicki said.

"We'll probably tell you some stuff that you don't need to know, too," Marci said, laughing. "Like, at lunch, avoid the Crispito."

Vicki nodded enthusiastically, making her hair bounce off her shoulders. "It tastes like donkey."

"And avoid the Idaho Haystack and the churro," Marci added. She stuck out her tongue and let it hang there.

"And the beef nuggets. I think they fry the churro and the beef nuggets in the same oil," Vicki said.

"Totally," Marci agreed. "The churros taste way beefy."

I nodded. "I'm used to gross and dangerous churros," I said. "I went to Sugar City Elementary."

"Bummer," Vicki said. "We went to Elm Grove Elementary in Texas. We had an all-weather track."

"Back to the cafeteria," Marci said.

"I was thinking I'd bring my lunch," I said.

Vicki and Marci looked at each other with a little bit of disgust and then looked at me and shook their heads.

"You definitely want to eat in the cafeteria and go through the lunch line. It's the easiest way to join a group." Marci pointed to herself. "I eat with the cheer-leaders."

Vicki pointed to Marci. "I eat with them too. They're great!"

"So I should eat with the cheerleaders?" I asked. Because it seemed like that's what they were suggesting, but it also seemed like I would have to be a cheerleader to do that.

"You can't," Marci said, puffing out her cheeks and look-ing disappointed. "Only the cheerleaders hang with the cheerleaders." She grabbed another piece of pizza and started chomping on it.

"I want to try out for the team," I said.

Marci and Vicki looked at each other and then at me. "It's a squad," Vicki said, grabbing her own slice of pizza. "And it's really hard for sixth graders to get on it. We only take, like, two, and they're generally expert gymnasts who are freakishly flexible. Can you do a back handspring or a strong series of round-offs?"

"No," I said. Then I took a huge bite of pizza.

"How are your backbends?" Marci asked. "Can you do a kickover to get out?"

I had never heard of a kickover. "Not quite."

"Well," Marci said, "you should probably focus on other groups."

"I want to try out for chorus," I said.

Vicki's eyes bugged out. "That's so cool! I was in chorus before I became the bee."

"Did you love it?" I asked.

Vicki shook her head. "It took up a lot of time. You have to practice after school. And you've got to travel. And a lot of snobs are in there."

"Oh," I said. Traveling sounded fun, but I didn't want to be around a bunch of snobs.

"Remember when Dolan was in the back row and he got sick during the Holiday Pageant and puked on everybody in front of him?" Marci asked.

"Ugh," Vicki said, nodding. "The whole gym smelled like barf for a week. By the way, he's still in chorus, so if you do make it, request to stand on the opposite side of him."

"What's his name again?" I asked.

"Dolan!" Vicki said, laughing a little.

"Vicki, you're making chorus sound totally lame, and it's not," Marci said. "But I do think this year's costumes involve red bow ties. Even for the girls."

"Good to know," I said. In my mind I was taking notes. *Avoid Crispitos and Dolan the Puker.*

"We're making middle school sound awful," Marci said. "Let's stick to the good stuff." They chewed their pizza more.

"Vending machines!" Vicki said. "They sell tons of junk

food and pop. Some schools have banned these items, but ours hasn't. It's awesome!"

"Chicken Patty and Tots Day for lunch," Marci said. "Don't miss it for anything. I had bronchitis once and I went to school just to get my patty and tots."

Marci nodded. "They're awesome."

Vicki and Marci looked at each other. "I'm going to miss some of this stuff," Marci said.

"I know. I'm not going to be the bee anymore," Vicki said, looking sad. "And that was, like, the highlight of my life. Stirring the crowd. Rallying the team. Wiggling my stinger-butt at the opposing bench."

Suddenly, Vicki looked sad.

"Sounds like you really enjoyed the costume," I said.

Vicki sighed. "When I was the bee, inside all that felt and fur, it was like the whole world loved me. And that's the best feeling ever."

"Are you moving back to Texas?" I asked. Even though I wasn't going to be able to sit with them at the cheer-leading table, I'd figured I would still be able to wave to them in the hallways and not feel totally lonely.

"We're ninth graders," Vicki said.

"We've graduated," Marci added.

Why my mother had set up a lunch date for me with two people in high school I had no idea. Then I sat and listened while Vicki and Marci talked about how much they were going to miss Pajama Fridays.

"At first I was like, I don't want to wear my pajamas to school!" Vicki said. "But it's a totally rocking time."

"I get to wear my pajamas to school on Fridays?" I asked. That seemed weird. I slept in boxer shorts. But I didn't tell them that.

"Once a month they hold a movie night in the gym and you get to wear your pajamas," Marci said.

"Should we tell her where to sit?" Vicki asked.

Marci nodded enthusiastically.

"Under the home-team hoop," Vicki said.

"Okay," I said. But again, I worried that maybe that was where the cheerleaders sat. And I wasn't certain I could be one of those. Because I didn't consider myself an expert gymnast or freakishly flexible.

"Do you have any questions for us?" Vicki asked. "Maybe about your teachers or the PE dress code?"

I hadn't thought about asking them about my teachers. And I didn't even know there was a PE dress code. I wondered if Sylvie had heard about that.

"I do have a question," I said.

"Is it about Mrs. Wahrwold's hair?" Vicki asked. "Because the rumors are true. It's a wig!"

I hadn't heard about Mrs. Wahrwold or her wig.

"It's about the T," I said.

Marci and Vicki looked at each other and then looked at me in an alarmed way.

"Is it true that kids try to lure other kids to the T and beat them up?" I asked.

And to my surprise—and horror—both Marci and Vicki nodded.

"Okay," Marci said. "We didn't want to scare you, but we should probably mention the psycho-bullies."

I gasped. I feared that there might be bullies in middle school, but I had no idea they'd be psycho.

"Cola and Beacher are seventh graders. And they're mean and awful and you should avoid them every day of your life," Vicki said. "They'll probably get expelled before Halloween."

"So there are only two psycho-bullies?" I asked. Because I felt like I could avoid two.

Vicki and Marci looked at each other again and then they looked at me, even more horrified than the first time.

"Cola has a brother. He's starting middle school this year," Vicki said. "He's supposed to be the worst of the worst."

"I've heard that he's done time in a juvenile detention center," Marci said.

"For what?" I asked.

Marci leaned over the table at me and practically spat her answer, "For being psycho."

Vicki shuddered. "Watch out." She pointed at me and it made the hair on my arms stand up.

"Are you sure the psycho-bullies won't be going to South?" I asked. It seemed like I had a fifty-fifty chance of avoiding them.

"All three psycho-bullies are going to North," Vicki said. "I'm certain."

"What are their names again?" I asked. I felt my throat growing tighter.

"Cola, Beacher, and Redge," Vicki said.

*Cola, Beacher, and Redge.*

Even their names sounded psycho.

"Uh-oh," Marci said. "We've scared Bessica. She's turning a weird color."

"I am?" I asked. Because I'd never turned a weird color before.

"Don't turn a weird color," Vicki said. "You'll be fine. Just avoid them in the halls. And avoid them at lunch. And never get close to the T."

"Good advice," Marci said, patting Vicki on the shoulder. "And hopefully you'll be fine."

"Hopefully?" I repeated.

"Should we tell her?" Marci asked.

Vicki shook her head. "No. Why scare her even more? Bessica isn't going to get mixed up with the alt crowd."

I felt my heart beating very fast. Sylvie and I had heard of the alt crowd. We'd seen them at the mall. They wore a lot of black and liked to pierce their ears and eyebrows and lips. Also, they smelled like motor oil.

"Don't mess with the alt crowd," Marci said. "You don't want any of them as your friends. You don't want any of them as your enemies."

"Don't even look them in the eye," Vicki said.

Then Marci pointed her finger at me and said in a very low and serious voice, "And stay away from the row."

"The row?" I asked.

Vicki squeezed her eyes shut and shuddered while her sister talked about the row. "It's the hallway that leads to metal shop. Half the lightbulbs are burnt out and everybody who hangs out there is a potential criminal. Only the *altest* of the alt go there."

I was surprised that the school would even have a hallway like that. But I didn't have a chance to ask more questions about it. Because Marci and Vicki talked about how excited they were to start high school. It was hard for me to pay total attention. Because my mind kept leaping to the terrible churros and alt crowd and psycho-bullies.

When we were finished eating pizza, my mom came in and offered us dessert. But Vicki and Marci couldn't stay.

They needed to drive to Rexburg and shop at the mall there.

"Did you guys exchange phone numbers?" my mom asked.

My mom handed me my cell phone. As Vicki and Marci rattled off their numbers, I loaded them into my contacts. But I didn't know why. Because I couldn't imagine calling these two. Ever.

I felt fuzzy and bummed out for the rest of the day. I kept my phone tucked in my pocket and I thought about calling Sylvie four thousand times. I wanted to warn her about the Crispito; I was pretty sure South had the same food as North. And I wanted to let her know about the dress code in PE. But that night, instead of calling my best friend and having a great conversation, I packed my back-pack and picked out my clothes. And then I got in my bed and let my mind swim for an hour. The house felt very empty without Grandma. I didn't hear her laugh. Or her voice. Or her terrible Frank Sinatra songs. I listened hard for all the sounds I missed. There was so much emptiness at one point that I thought I started to hear the ocean. And the next thing I knew, I had the weirdest dream of my life.

The weirdest dream of my life was short and terrible. I was in the middle-school bathroom. I recognized it from orientation. For some reason, I was standing in there and missing all my classes. Girl after girl came in to use the bathroom. But none of them talked to me. Sometimes I gave them paper towels after they washed their hands. A few of the girls came in laughing with their friends, *ha, ha, ha.* But I didn't laugh. Because nobody told me the joke. I was very nervous about missing all my classes. But, weirdly enough, not nervous enough to leave the bathroom.

Lots of girls kept cramming their way into the bathroom. Girl after girl after girl. They all seemed to know each other. Then the PE teacher showed up, and she made us do exercises. And I didn't want to fail PE. So I did them. Jumping jacks. Squats. Push-ups. Then the cheerleaders showed up. And surrounded me. The whole squad. And they did cheerleader things, like flips and bends. I was afraid one of them would end up in the toilet. Or bang her head on a faucet. But they were very coordinated and that didn't happen.

Then Principal Tidge showed up. And she stood right next to me. And nobody else thought this was weird, so I didn't say anything. And Principal Tidge started doing exercises too. And the PE teacher yelled at us to jog. So we did. *Jog. Jog. Jog.* Even Principal Tidge. Then I saw Sylvie. I was shocked! Because she didn't even say hello. And she was jogging too. Then I heard laughing. Why were people laughing? And then I realized they were pointing at me. Even Principal Tidge!

"What's her name?" somebody asked.

"Bessica Lefter!" Sylvie said.

I couldn't believe Sylvie did that. I couldn't believe that Sylvie would tell all these bathroom laughers my name.

Then Principal Tidge was laughing so hard that she tipped over.

Then I woke up. But I wasn't laughing. I was so hot I was sweating. I kicked the covers off me and stared into the darkness. This was the first dream I'd ever had where Sylvie acted like a complete jerk. I didn't understand what it meant. I closed my eyes again. But I never totally fell back asleep.

# THINGS TO DO IN MIDDLE SCHOOL

1. Avoid Psycho-bullies, Crispitos, and Dolan the Puker
2. Attend my classes in the correct order:
   Nutrition
   English
   Math
   Lunch
   Geography
   Public Speaking
   PE

3. Continue boyfriend search for Grandma
4. Try to stop hating Sylvie (even in my dreams)
5. Find a lunch group
6. Learn

# CHAPTER

When my mom poked her head into my room and told me that it was time to get up, I couldn't believe it was already morning. Partly because I felt like I hadn't slept enough. And partly because it was still dark outside and I could hear Dad snoring like a lawn mower.

I stared at the ceiling and tried to remember how to get from one class to the next. Because maybe that was why I'd stayed in the bathroom during my dream. I knew where to go for PE, because the gym was in the center of the school. But things got a little fuzzy for me after that. There were so many things to remember and keep straight. *Too many*. Psycho-bullies. Hallways. Teachers. Classrooms. Bathrooms. Dolan the Puker. My locker. Beef nuggets . . .

"It's time to get up," my mom said again. Then she flipped on my light and blinded me.

Sitting up in bed, covering my eyes, I suddenly felt two different ways about school. I really wanted to go to school. I really didn't want to go to school.

But I got out of bed anyway. At first, nothing was different. I already had my outfit picked out. I put on a pink shirt and jeans and attached the pink tongues to my sneakers. Then, I got ready exactly the same way that I'd gotten ready for elementary school. But my stomach felt very queasy. Because after I left my house, I sort of had no idea what would happen next. I peeked out my curtain into my front yard. Outside, it was still pitch black. And this freaked me out a little. Because I didn't know whether I could get up this early for a whole year.

When I sat down to eat breakfast, I saw a tiny box with a bow on it.

"It's for good luck," my mom said.

This worried me a little bit, because it was like my mom already knew that things were going to be rocky for me at North Teton Middle School and that I would need luck. I lifted the top off and stared down at a pink bracelet. It was really spectacular. Too bad I couldn't show it to Sylvie.

"Thanks," I said. I slid the pink beads over my hand and settled the bracelet on my wrist. Then I looked at the clock to make sure I wouldn't miss the bus.

"Don't worry," my mom said. "You've got plenty of time."

I finished eating and put on my backpack. With all of my supplies in it, that thing was so heavy it made me tip a little. Then I realized that I should not have practiced wearing it empty in front of my mirror; I should have practiced wearing it stuffed with heavy items. Because from what I knew thus far in my life about teachers and homework, my backpack would only get heavier by the end of the day.

"You're not taking your phone, right?" my mom asked.

"I am," I said.

My mother frowned. "What if you drop it? You're not even allowed to use it at school."

I glanced at my phone. Why did my mom think I would drop it? That was a rude thing to think. Then, while I was looking at it, something cool happened. It started to ring.

"Who is it?" my mom asked. But the way she asked the question made it sound like she already knew.

I read the number. "It's Grandma!"

"How exciting!" my mother said.

And it was exciting. I hadn't talked to her since she'd fled my life to be with Willy.

**Me:** Grandma! Where are you?

**Grandma:** We made it through Nebraska. We should be in Minnesota tomorrow.

**Me:** That's a bummer.

**Grandma:** It's not a bummer. Willy and I are having a great time!

**Me:** Oh. (pause) I miss you.

**Grandma:** I miss you, too, doll. And I want you to have a great day at school. I bet you'll make a thousand friends.

**Me:** That's unlikely, because my school doesn't even have a thousand people in it.

**Grandma:** I was speaking hyperbolically.

**Me:** Hyper what?

**Grandma:** Maybe you should look it up in your pocket dictionary.

**Me:** Okay.

So I slipped off my backpack and unzipped it and pulled out my pink pocket dictionary.

> **Me:** My dictionary doesn't have that word. How do you spell it?
>
> **Mom:** Is Grandma playing a spelling game with you? I don't think you have time for that.
>
> **Me:** But I need to know what *hyperbolically* means or I'll be distracted all day.
>
> **Grandma:** Look up *hyperbole*. H-Y-P-E-R-B-O-L-E.
>
> **Me:** *A deliberate exaggeration used for effect.* Well, I knew you were exaggerating, I just didn't know what *hyperbolically* meant.
>
> **Grandma:** Now you do.
>
> **Me:** When do you enter your first cave?
>
> **Mom:** You don't have time for a conversation. This was supposed to be a pep talk.
>
> **Me:** Excuse me, Mom, but Grandma is still pepping me.
>
> **Grandma:** It sounds like you have to go, Bessica.

But I was having a pretty good conversation, and I wasn't totally ready to leave my house and get on a school bus and go to middle school and face all those hazards. I probably would have felt differently if Sylvie was on my bus. But that wasn't going to be my reality.

Then my mom took away the phone.

> **MOM:** She's going to miss the bus. Can she call you after school?

Then my mother looked at me. "Put on your backpack. You might need to run."

I put on my backpack, but I didn't think I wanted to run. Because everybody on my bus would see me doing that. And I hadn't practiced running in my backpack; I'd only practiced standing in front of my mirror. What if I looked stupid?

"Are you still talking to Grandma?" I asked, pointing to my phone.

My mom snapped my phone closed. "She'll call you later."

Instead of handing me my phone, she set it on the mail-sorting table by the front door. Then I felt my mom pushing on my shoulder. "The bus!"

"Don't shove me," I said. "I'm top-heavy. I'll tip."

"But you don't want to miss it!" my mom said.

I didn't know whether that was a true statement. My mom gave me another push and I guess her panic was contagious, because I hurried out the door and took off running like a crazy person. But I didn't run very far. Because it was too late. The bus had already passed my house.

My mom walked outside and stood beneath our porch light and stared at me.

"I just missed the bus," I said.

"Let me tell Dad that I'm driving you."

So on the first day, my mom drove me to school. But as she cruised down the road, I became very worried about something. Would my mother driving me to school make me look like a baby? Or a wimp? Or a dweeb? Or some sort of baby-wimp-dweeb combo? I didn't want that.

"Do you want me to drop you near the T?" she asked.

It was like my mom and I weren't even on the same team anymore. Why would I want that? "No!" I yelled.

My mother glanced over at me with a very confused expression.

My stomach flipped over and over. I still felt two ways about school. I wanted to go to school worse than anything. And worse than anything, I didn't want to go to school. I sort of wanted my mom to keep driving. Maybe all the way to Canada. Then it happened! I could see the school. And I didn't want to see the school. Then I could see the kids outside the school. Then I could see the T!

I began to breathe very fast as my mother passed a school bus. It looked crowded. I could see people laughing behind the rectangle windows. This was not good. I'd really blown it. Because the bus ride might have been an excellent friendship-building opportunity, whereas having your mother drop you off near the T could get you killed.

"You can let me out here," I said.

But my mom was still driving thirty miles per hour.

"Don't take me to the T," I begged.

"Okay. I'll pull into the drive," she said.

But when I looked at the drive, it was lined with buses. And there was a Bus Only sign at the top of the drive.

"It's Bus Only!" I said. "Don't park here!" I didn't want my mom parking in the wrong place so everybody would stare at me when I got out of the car.

But my mother stopped the car.

"I'm sure they don't mind," she said. "It's your first day."

I felt my mom leaning toward me. I looked at her and saw a pair of puckered lips closing in on me. "Mom!" I said. "You can't kiss me in front of the whole school." I pointed out my window at the school.

"Okay. Bye." She pulled back and waved.

"Bye," I said. Then I swallowed hard and hurried out of the car. I hustled across the lawn in the darkness; my backpack really slowed me down. For the next year, until the new school was built, day classes would start at six-thirty in the morning. I didn't know how I was going to survive. Sylvie's classes didn't start until one o'clock in the afternoon. But she didn't get out of school until it was almost night. I was halfway to the building when I heard something I didn't want to hear.

"Look at that sixth grader run!" a boy yelled.

And I realized he might have been talking about me, so I slowed down. But he said something else.

"Now she doesn't want to run anymore," the boy said. "Too bad. She was funny to watch."

And then I heard people laughing and it cut through me. I didn't want people laughing at me. That was not why I'd come to middle school. And that was when it hit me! I was being teased. I had seen on a talk show once that if you didn't stand up to the person who was teasing you right away, you would be teased until you moved away. And both my parents liked their jobs and we didn't have any plans to move. So I needed to stand up for myself. I turned toward the teaser and acted like I wasn't afraid. Even though I was.

"Sometimes I run. Sometimes I walk," I said. "It's a free country."

And then he did this awful thing where he walked toward me and he said in a fake girl voice, "Sometimes I run and sometimes I walk. It's a free country." Then he made a growling noise for no reason at all.

I wanted him to stop. Because I hadn't come to middle school to get growled at either. I'd come to middle school to take six classes and possibly become a cheerleader and chorus member and join other exciting groups and make a bunch of friends.

But the teaser kept growling at me. And then I realized I wasn't standing where most of the other kids were standing. Somehow I'd drifted and I wasn't anywhere near the front door of the school. I was off to the side. I'd been lured to the T! I looked around in horror. That was when I saw the red marks on the ground. They could have been paint, but to me they looked like dried puddles of blood. I felt very afraid. I breathed so quickly that I thought I was going to suck in too much air and make my lungs pop like balloons.

The boy walked closer to me.

And instead of walking away or saying something more to stand up for myself, I yelled, "It's the T!"

Apparently, school staff were aware of the T's reputation, because a teacher named Mrs. Hackett appeared out of nowhere. And she started yelling at the teaser and his two friends.

"Who's causing problems?" Mrs. Hackett asked. Then she glared at them. And then she looked at me.

Then I figured that growling was basically the same thing as causing problems, so I pointed at the boy who'd done that.

She put her hand on my shoulder and it looked a lot like a man's hand. It had hair on it and everything. And then I noticed that Mrs. Hackett had goggles dangling around her neck. Also, she smelled like diesel fuel. I looked up at her and then back at the jerk-boys. I kept pointing at the growler—a tall, thin blond kid who was wearing baggy jeans.

"We were just talking!" the boy said.

"All right, Cola, remember what you were told last year after the pushpin/water balloon fiasco. Any subsequent disruption—even the tiniest infraction—would result in a visit to the principal's office. You know the way," Mrs. Hackett said.

I couldn't believe it. I gasped and covered my mouth with my hand. I hadn't even made it inside the building yet and I'd encountered a psycho-bully. I glanced at the other two boys. Then it hit me. *These must be the other two psycho-bullies!* My knees felt very shaky, and the other two psycho-bullies shot me very hateful looks. It made me feel terrible. In fact, I felt terrible about my whole morning.

By the time Cola the psycho-bully got hauled away, there

weren't many people outside anymore. And I became very worried that I was going to be tardy for nutrition. So I hurried as fast as I could into the building. That was when I saw all the club posters. They hadn't been there at orientation. The papers were taped to the walls. Green posters. Orange posters. Blue posters. Yellow posters. Pink posters.

There were so many clubs. There was one for chorus. And cheerleading. And a book club. I pulled off the posters I found interesting as fast as I could, because they contained all the information about where and when the clubs met. And that was useful information that was hard to remember. Even though it seemed like a long shot, I even took a poster about a math club.

"Hey!" said a girl. "Those are nonremovable."

She was so tall that I knew right away that she was a seventh or possibly eighth grader. But what she was saying didn't make much sense, because I'd found the posters very removable. They were only held up with tape.

She stood there with her straight-across bangs and long brown hair, waiting for me to say something. But I didn't. "They are posted with the School Approved stamp," the girl explained. "You're not allowed to take down official signs."

I looked at the pile of posters. "Official signs?" They didn't look all that official. They looked like I could make them at home on my computer.

"You need to put them back up," the girl said.

"But I don't have any tape," I told her. "And I'll be late for class."

She held her hand out like she wanted me to give her the posters. She seemed so bossy and unkind about it. I wondered if maybe she was a psycho-bully too.

"What's your name?" she asked.

But I didn't answer her, because in this situation I preferred to remain anonymous.

"My name is Cameron Bon Qui Qui. I'm a hall monitor. When I ask questions you have to answer them. I have that kind of authority."

And so I handed her the posters, even though I needed that information. Then I turned around and started hustling toward my locker.

"Hey," Cameron Bon Qui Qui said. "I need to know your name. Plus, you can't run in the hallways. Slow down or I'll report you."

I slowed down a little, but not because I wanted to slow down. There were so many bodies in the hallway that it was tough to get around them all. Also, a lot of them seemed lost. I kept moving, winding around their bulging backpacks. I heard Cameron Bon Qui Qui's footsteps behind me. I wanted her to leave me alone and let me find my locker.

"Stop!" Cameron Bon Qui Qui said. "When a hall

monitor says 'stop' you have to stop. It's in our middle-school constitution!"

I was surprised to hear that my middle school had one of those, or that I would be expected to honor it without even knowing what it said. So then I started running again, and I didn't even try to open my stupid locker. In fact, I didn't even remember where my stupid locker was. I hurried up the stairs and ducked into room 204, which was where I was supposed to be for my first class, nutrition. I found a seat in the corner and I put my head down on my desk.

I heard Cameron Bon Qui Qui's shoes squeak past room 204.

"I'm looking for a violator," she said. "She has short brown hair."

Then a bell rang.

"Just go to class," a voice in the hallway said. It sounded like a grown-up, but I couldn't see her. "Lots of people are violators on the first day." It was a woman wearing a red fluffy sweater and red cowboy boots. She looked like a cowgirl. She had a shiny belt buckle, but it wasn't nearly as big as Willy's. Then she walked into the room and shut the door.

I lifted up my head and looked around. So this was nutrition. I thought maybe we'd study apples or good posture. But I really had no idea. I glanced around the room.

All the nice kids seemed to be sitting at the front. And here I was, sitting next to kids who looked like they vandalized the vending machines on a regular basis. As soon as I had a chance to move seats, I was going to take it.

"I am Mrs. Mounds," the teacher said. She wrote her name on the dry-erase board in big pink letters. "Look around. Where you are seated today will be your permanent seat."

I looked around and then I almost puked. I couldn't believe what I saw. One of the psycho-bullies from the T incident was in my class and he was sitting right next to me. He scowled at me and I looked back up to the front of the room. If I were sitting in the middle of the class, I'd be closer to more people and have a better chance of making friends. This was lame. I smiled at a tough-looking girl who was wearing a football jersey over her shirt. She didn't smile back. She looked at me like she'd already decided that she didn't want to like me. And I had no idea why that was.

"As many of you may know, this is your homeroom," Mrs. Mounds said.

I had never had a homeroom before.

"This class is ten minutes longer than your other classes," Mrs. Mounds said.

I pulled out my schedule and checked this out. She was right.

"It's a time for official school announcements, which is how each day will start."

Then a voice boomed into our room from a speaker on the wall.

"Good morning! I'm Principal Tidge! Welcome to North Teton Middle School! In case some of you missed orientation, I'm going to go through some useful information."

Then Principal Tidge repeated a lot of information that I already knew. She even repeated the banned-weapons list, which was a downer to hear first thing in the morning. I was pretty happy when she got to the end.

"I want you to have a great day! And remember to be kind to the sixth graders! See you in the hallways!"

From across the hallway I could hear people laughing. Then I heard a boy yell, "I'm gonna smash a sixth grader just like this!" Then I heard a terrible thumping sound, and the laughter got really loud. But nobody in our room laughed. Because we were all sixth graders.

I watched Mrs. Mounds write her email address on the board, next to a list of rules. She had a lot of rules. We couldn't be late. Or eat or drink. Or use any electronic equipment. We couldn't talk. And we had to sit in the same desk each time. And we got a zero on all late work. And if we cheated on anything we'd fail. Also, she had a rule that we couldn't pass gas, which I guess made sense.

I'd just never seen it as a written rule before. Some kids laughed when she read that one.

"She means we can't fart," the psycho-bully said to another kid.

"She must have big-time farting problems," the kid said. Then he made a very quiet farting noise and he and the psycho-bully snickered.

"Listen up," Mrs. Mounds said. "No talking while I'm talking."

After everybody was quiet again, Mrs. Mounds handed us information cards to fill out and I unzipped my backpack to get a pen. When Mrs. Mounds heard my zipper, she looked at me.

"Backpacks have to be stored in your locker," she said. "In the hallways they're bumping hazards. In the classroom they're tripping hazards."

"I know," I said. I looked down at my backpack. It was halfway in the aisle and I felt bad about that. I thought maybe she was going to force me to leave class and put my hazardous backpack in my locker. But she didn't.

"Make sure you put it in your locker before the next class," she said.

"Okay." I thought about explaining my morning to her, but I didn't want everybody in nutrition listening. So I tried to pull my backpack out of the aisle, and I shoved it so far underneath my desk that I put my feet on top of it and I felt very cramped. I carefully reached inside my un-zipped compartment for a pen. Then the psycho-bully bumped me on the arm and asked if I had another pen. I turned to face him and we locked eyes. And in his pupils I could see little images of my own face. And I looked scared.

"Here," I said. I handed him a blue pen.

"I'm not giving this back," he said. "I'm keeping it. And I want you to bring me a pen tomorrow too."

And then I watched the little images of myself nod, which suggested I was okay with this arrangement.

"My name is Redge," he said. "You sent my brother Cola to the principal today. And he didn't even deserve it. Sometimes Cola does deserve it, but today he didn't. Now me and Cola and Beacher are going to punish you."

I blinked.

"You're a rat," Redge said.

"I am not," I said, because even though I was scared and uncomfortable with where things were headed with Redge, I thought I should defend myself.

Redge smirked at me.

"No talking while I'm talking," Mrs. Mounds said. Then she walked to the top of my row. "What's your name in the back?"

I looked behind me, but it was just the wall.

"With the backpack," she added.

Oh no. "Bessica," I said.

She looked down at her roll book. "Bessica Lefter?" she asked.

I nodded.

Then she turned around and walked to the wipe board and wrote down my name. *My name*. And she didn't even use pink marker. She used brown. Then she wrote Redge Marzo's name on the board.

"If you get a check next to your name, you lose ten points," Mrs. Mounds said.

"From what?" I asked.

"Your first assignment," she said.

And I felt my eyes get warm and my throat get lumpy. Because I didn't like what I was hearing. I'd started my first class in middle school in the hole, down a pen, stuck in the corner next to a psycho-bully.

I reached down and touched my pink bracelet over and over. I tried to be optimistic. *Middle school can only improve*, I told myself. *You'll meet nice people in your next class. You'll bump into a ton of cool people by lunch. You'll probably end up in a fascinating lunch group. You'll probably even like PE.*

But I was wrong about that.

# CHAPTER

**11**

**M**iddle school did not get any better. That first day was pretty terrible. Mrs. Mounds spent a bunch of time discussing what was in food, gram by gram.

"A grapefruit has sixteen grams of sugar and four grams of dietary fiber.

"An order of medium French fries from McDonald's has nineteen grams of fat."

I wrote down as much of this as I could in my notebook. And when the bell rang, I hurried to my locker to dump off my backpack. But my combination was very hard to remember. I tried once. Twice. Three times. *Yank. Yank. Yank.* My locker really enjoyed being locked. I looked at the clock on the wall. A flood of people zoomed past me. Then I decided to forget about my locker and take my hazardous backpack and head straight to English. I wanted a seat near the front.

Mr. Val welcomed us by playing some sort of ancient music that had a flute in it. He greeted us at the door and made little bows when we walked past him. He said he was trying to establish a mood. And I liked that idea, even though I didn't like the ancient flute music. Happily, he didn't say anything about my backpack. And so I picked out a seat near the front and stuffed it underneath me. Sort of.

Mr. Val was the tallest teacher I'd had in my life. He looked younger than my parents. I didn't know what to expect from a tall, young, flute-loving teacher, but I soon learned. He was all about work. As he took roll, he made us come to the front of the class and get our assigned textbooks.

"You'll need to put a cover on them by Friday. We don't want to end a book's life prematurely," he said as the first boy, Toby Alda, collected his book. I got my book somewhere in the middle of everybody and sat down and flipped through it. There were assignments at the end of every unit. Bleh.

"Let's read the preface together," Mr. Val said. He half sat on his desk and started reading. " 'The essentials of

English grammar can be broken down into thirty-six categories.' "

And this really cut into my ability to be social or make friends, because after the preface, Mr. Val immediately started to "refresh our memories" about language. Which required a lot of writing and rule-remembering about parts of speech, which I couldn't remember all that well. Because that wasn't the sort of thing that Sylvie and I talked about over the summer. Also, he announced that we would have something called permanent homework. Which meant that he would hand us a poem to take home every Monday, Wednesday, and Friday and that we had to read it at home four times in our heads and one time out loud and then write a response paragraph. I'd never had to write one of those before.

"You will be responding to poems written by some of the best poets of yesterday and today," he said. "Wordsworth! Keats! Bishop! Millay! Frost!" He sounded so excited. But I wasn't. Because permanent homework felt like a drag. And instead of making friends and solidifying a lunch group, I had to remember what nouns were. And verbs. And Mr. Val also expected us to remember modifiers, prepositions, and articles (of both the definite and indefinite variety). It was impossible. And he never turned off the flute music.

By the time I left English and walked to math, I felt so

fuzzy, I had a hard time concentrating or finding my class-room. And once I got there, I had a tough time staying awake. I was so sleepy that I didn't even pick out my seat strategically. I just sat in an empty desk in the middle of the class. Luckily, I ended up next to a girl who had a pretty good smile. Also, she had dimples, and I liked those on people. But I never actually talked to her, and the whole class was very forgettable. It was just numbers and problems. When the bell rang and I left, I couldn't even re-member what my math teacher looked like. He may have been wearing a hat.

There I was. It was time for lunch. Everybody streamed down the hallway in the direction of the cafeteria. I didn't have a group of friends or a single friend or a random ac-quaintance to partner up with. It was the biggest bummer ever. When this happens, it's pretty obvious to everyone, even yourself, that you are alone and don't have anybody.

I walked toward my locker and thought about the odor girl from the library. And then it was like I could predict the future, because after I thought of her, she walked right past me with a group of friends. But I didn't notice an odor. She smiled at me, but I didn't want to eat with the odor girl and her friends, so I kept walking toward my locker and hoping that a miracle would happen. And then a miracle did happen, because somebody from my tap-dance clinic recognized me.

"Bessica Lefter!" she said. She was short and blond and had big ears and a round face.

"Hi," I said.

"I'm me! Annabelle Deeter!" And she hurried up to me and started asking me all these questions about what I'd done since tap dance. I didn't know how to answer them. Because I barely remembered tap dance. Sylvie and I mostly talked about my gorgeous neighbor Noll Beck in there. Also, we tapped a lot.

"Is Sylvie here?" Annabelle gushed. "She had the best buffalo pullback."

I stared at Annabelle and decided to ignore some of what she was asking. Because I didn't remember Sylvie ever doing anything buffalo-like ever. "Sylvie went to South." And then even though I didn't really know Annabelle, I wanted Annabelle to invite me to lunch with her.

"We're headed to the cafeteria!" Annabelle said. She looked so excited. Sort of manic. And I didn't know why. Then she waved to a group of girls. "Do you want to sit with us?"

And I was so grateful, I accepted right away.

"Yes," I said.

"Do you want to put your backpack away first? We'll wait," Annabelle said.

But I worried that I wouldn't be able to get my locker

open. And I worried that if I took too long, these people might leave me. So I declined.

"I'll bring it," I said.

We walked in one big clump to the cafeteria.

"Bessica was in my tap clinic. So was her friend, Sylvie. She was the best tapper in the class," Annabelle told her friends while we walked.

This surprised me. Because I hadn't realized that Sylvie had been the best tapper. It had been her first class. But after Annabelle brought this up, it was like I couldn't get Sylvie out of my mind. *Tap. Tap. Tap.* Her favorite step was the crisscross cramp roll. Step. Dig. Heel. Toe. Step. Dig. Heel. Toe. Sometimes, when I was bored, she'd even do that move for me in my kitchen. I followed Annabelle.

"That is so sad that you two got separated," Annabelle said. She made a big frowning face.

"Yeah," I said. I really hoped she'd stop talking about Sylvie. Because it was making me miss her. A lot.

All the other girls chatted about their classes. Unlike Sylvie and me, who just had each other, these girls seemed to be in a big network of best friends. And instead of wanting to join their network, I found myself really wanting Sylvie. I wondered what would happen if I called her from school. She was probably at home. In fact, she was probably thinking about me!

I was superbummed that my phone was sitting at home on the mail-sorting table, where I couldn't use it. I looked around at the happy chatting girls. I needed to call Sylvie *immediately*. But I also needed to establish my lunch group. And as I was trying to figure out a way to do both, I got stopped at the door. Mrs. Hackett, the teacher from this morning, was standing guard, and she said, "Backpacks aren't allowed in the cafeteria."

Annabelle turned and looked at me.

"Come on," her friends said.

"We'll be right over there," she said. I glanced at the table where she was pointing. Then I glanced at the menu posted next to the door. They were serving Crispitos. And then Annabelle and her friends walked away and left me at the door.

I didn't know exactly what to do, so I took my violating backpack and walked as fast as I could down the hall. I figured I'd try my locker one more time. And then come back.

When I got to my locker, I spotted something I hadn't noticed before. On the locker next to mine there were stickers that spelled D-A-V-I-S. And I thought that was a smart idea, because I bet Davis had an easy time finding his locker because his name was stuck right on it. I didn't know if this made Davis a dweeb, a dork, or a normal person.

I kneeled down in front of my locker and turned it exactly toward the numbers. *Yank. Yank. Yank.* It opened! And as I was stuffing my backpack inside, I heard a slamming sound. I turned around and watched in horror as a group of boys lifted another boy off the ground and dumped him into a tall metal can. Once he was in there, I watched all the stuffer boys walk away. I couldn't stop staring. Then I realized that the kid in the trash can was Blake! And I felt horrible for him. Because in addition to his parents getting divorced, he was now stuck inside a garbage container.

"Are you okay?" I asked.

But he didn't answer me.

"Do you need help?" I asked. "Should I get a teacher? Or the nurse?"

But Blake rolled onto his side and tipped the trash can over so he could get out. And he never said anything. He picked up his books and walked away. And then I shut my locker. And I made sure it was locked. And then I hurried down the hallway to find Annabelle and her friends. When I got to the lunchroom again, I looked inside.

The voices bounced off the walls and floors. I glanced across the whole room. Face. Face. Face. Body. Body. Body. Tray. Tray. Tray. Table after table looked full. I couldn't see Annabelle. Was she still in line? I worried that if I didn't find a group right now, I would never be able to find one. And I worried this would make me look like a loser. But wandering around alone in the cafeteria would make me look like a loser too. It felt like all my options were loser choices. I looked and looked and looked. Then I caught Redge the psycho-bully glaring at me from his table, so I left.

I figured I would find a vending machine and eat, and then go track down my geography classroom and try to secure my lunch group tomorrow. I found a vending machine that offered a variety of corn chips and cookies. They looked good. I pulled some quarters out of my pocket and fed them into the machine. That was when I realized who I was surrounded by. This place was crawling with the alt crowd. I thought about leaving. But I needed to eat something and I really wanted cookies. It bummed me out to think that I was eating in the area where people who didn't want friends ate. Because I did want friends. I just wasn't sure how to make them.

I pressed the buttons for the cookies and waited for them to drop. I hadn't planned on buying a lunch that contained zero nutrition. But I did. I reached into the machine's tray and took my cookies, and instead of going to the cafeteria and figuring out how to make friends, I walked to the row beside the stairs where some of the alt crowd ate. And I stood at the ledge. All by myself. And opened my cookies. And I ate them too.

I didn't talk to the alt crowd. That was part of what made them alts. They didn't talk to each other. And as I ate my cookies, I didn't try to fool myself into thinking my day was going to get better. I ate my cookies and tried to convince myself that I wasn't going to die.

And in my after-lunch class, geography, we weren't studying beaches like I'd hoped, because Mr. Hoser, my geography teacher, was obsessed with polar regions. He wore a tie with a picture of a glacier on it and promised us a virtual field trip to Antarctica, brought to us by NASA TV. And while some kids clapped, I did not find this to be a thrilling concept. Public speaking was pretty awful too. Mrs. Moppett kicked off class by telling everybody that our major assignment of the semester would be to give a speech in front of the whole class on an assigned topic about politics. And the psycho-bully Redge Marzo was in there with me again. And the only good thing I can say about that particular psycho-bully was that he managed to hang on to the pen I gave him in nutrition, so I didn't have to give him two pens a day.

And my last class of the day, PE, which I knew was going to be puke-bad, was just as terrible as I had feared. My PE teacher, Ms. Penrod, took her job very seriously. Ms. Penrod used to be an Olympian. She'd thrown a shot put in the games in Korea, but she hadn't won any medals. And I could tell right away that she was still bummed out about it. And would most likely punish us for an entire semester. Also, the PE dress code required us to wear school colors. Which meant I was going to have to track down a pair of either purple or gold pants.

When the last bell finally rang and I went out to catch the bus, I was so tired that I thought I was going to fall asleep and miss my stop. But that didn't happen. Because I sat near the front and watched closely out the window for my house. When I saw it, I jumped up. I think I frightened the person next to me, but I didn't really care. I hurried off the bus and ran inside and felt relieved that my first day of middle school was over.

# CHAPTER 12

I wasn't expecting my mom to be home. She always worked at the podiatrist's office until three o'clock. But she was home! As soon as I walked through the door, she started taking pictures of me.

"We didn't get a shot of you this morning," she said. I put my hands up and blocked my face. I was not in the mood for picture taking.

"Can't we do this tomorrow morning?" I asked. "When my pixie is fresh?" I pulled my hands down and she clicked another picture.

"Okay. Are you hungry?"

I nodded and slipped off my backpack and went to the kitchen, where I found my favorite sandwich already made. Turkey and pickles on sourdough.

"This one looks great," my mom said, showing me her camera.

I glanced at the screen. Inside the small square I looked very tired and surprised, and my pixie looked totally flat.

"That's the first time I've seen what my hair looks like in a picture," I said. "It's short. I mean, I got totally snipped!"

My mother nodded. "Luckily, it's cute." She took her camera back. "How was your day?"

And I thought about crying and telling her that it was a bummer, but I was starving. So I just grabbed my sandwich and started eating.

"Tell me about your classes!" my mom said.

But I didn't feel like reliving my day at all. I felt like forgetting it.

"Okay," my mom said. "Eat first and we can talk about it later."

I nodded.

"Your grandma sent you a postcard from South Dakota!" my mom said as she poured me a second glass of milk.

I swallowed. "Why is Grandma writing me from South Dakota? I thought she was going to Minnesota." And I thought maybe I could convince my mom that Willy really was a maniac welder and that he'd kidnapped Grandma and we had to get her back.

"Their route takes them through South Dakota," my mother said. "She's having the time of her life. It almost makes me want to rent a motor home for the summer."

I drank my milk and stared at her. I thought that sounded awful. "Motor homes are dangerous and they pollute the air."

My mom dusted some bread crumbs off the table.

"Your first day without Sylvie had to have been tough," she said.

I drank more of my milk and didn't say anything. Just because I hated motor homes didn't mean I was missing Sylvie. Which I was. "I've got homework."

"Do you need any help?"

I shook my head. "I need solitude. And pencils. And my backpack."

As I got all my stuff together, I considered telling my mom about the psycho-bullies and my difficult locker and all the other bummer things about my day. But she looked so tired. And she'd tried so hard to make me feel better. She'd even gotten off work early just to be here when I got home. I couldn't ruin her day just because mine had been terrible.

I sat on my bed and pulled out my English book because Mr. Val wanted us to preview a unit on future-tense verbs.

As I previewed it I could tell that it was not going to be my favorite unit. Also, I had to read a poem and respond to it. It was by Emily Dickinson, and it didn't even have a title. And I usually found titles to be very helpful. I read the poem to myself four times. Then I read it out loud. And I didn't whisper it. I belted it right out. Because I thought that might help me understand it.

> I'm nobody! Who are you?
> Are you nobody, too?
> Then there's a pair of us—don't tell!
> They'd banish us, you know.
>
> How dreary to be somebody!
> How public, like a frog.
> To tell your name the livelong day
> To an admiring bog!

Then I heard my mom call to me. "You are too somebody! You're Bessica Lefter!"

And I thought maybe I should tell my mom that I was doing my permanent homework, which happened to be a poem without a title, but I explained it in a shorter way. "I didn't write that!" Then I wrote my paragraph. Mr. Val said there were no wrong answers. So I took him at his word and wrote from the heart.

If you are a nobody and you are part of a pair, then you aren't a nobody anymore. I used to be part of a pair. I liked it. Because I never felt alone. I felt like I had a friend who understood everything about me, what made me happy, what bummed me out. And she was a good listener. And now she's one hundred percent out of my life. Because her mom is an evil eyelash painter who doesn't understand the concept of friendship. But maybe I don't totally understand the concept of friendship either. Because I made my friend throw away our diary when she didn't want to. And I also made her get a drastic haircut.

When I looked over my paragraph, I was surprised by how long it was. Also, I was surprised by its honesty. Because usually when I wrote things for school, I tried to write what I thought the teacher wanted to read. And in this case I hadn't done that; I'd written what was on my mind.

When I finished English, I broke out my math worksheets. I had to solve eight problems and they all looked terrible. And then I opened my nutrition notebook and reviewed the fat grams in various nuts. And then I decided I could do the rest of my homework while lying down. But that didn't turn out so good. Because the next thing I knew, it was dark outside and I could smell baking tuna fish.

I climbed off my bed and walked into the kitchen, and the table was set and my dad was all ready to eat.

"Hey there, sunshine," he said. "How was school?"

"Fine," I lied. Because I was still very groggy and didn't feel like getting into the horrible details also known as my day.

"Let's eat!" Mom said.

And I sat down pretty quickly. Because even though I'd eaten a turkey sandwich, I still felt like I could use more nourishment.

"Bessica has been in her room working on homework," my mom said.

My dad whistled. "Are they piling it on already?"

I nodded.

"I have permanent homework in English," I said. "And it's hard."

My dad whistled again.

"It will get easier once you get a rhythm down," my mom said.

I looked at her like she was crazy. That didn't even make sense.

"Did you see Blake today?" my dad asked.

"I sure did," I said. "He got stuffed into a trash can by my locker."

My mom set down a bowl of mashed potatoes on the table and gasped. "That's awful!"

I nodded. "But he got out okay."

"Did you help him?" my mom asked.

"He didn't want my help. He's a loner. I think that's part of why he got stuffed," I said.

"That doesn't surprise me," my dad said. "That kid is sort of a dweeb."

My mom frowned when my dad said that. "Buck, we shouldn't judge socially awkward children."

My dad spooned up some potatoes and said, "You're right."

"Do you want one or two scoops of peas?" my mom asked me.

"One," I said, because if I had a choice, I wanted to take the smallest amount of peas possible.

My mom finished dishing everything out and she sat down. Then I realized that I was looking at a pork chop but I still smelled baking tuna fish.

"Why do I smell tuna?" I asked.

My mom smiled. "Because I'm making a casserole for one of the patients."

This was something she did on a regular basis. My mom was not the kind of receptionist who could write down people's information and file it away. She was the kind of person who wrote down their information and then baked things to make them feel better.

"I want more details, Bessica. What was the first thing you thought when I dropped you off today?"

I blinked. And ate some peas. And swallowed them. "I thought, I would be enjoying my day a lot more if Sylvie were here."

My mother sighed. "Mrs. Potaski will come around. Give her time."

I shook my head. "No. Grandma explained it to me. Sylvie's mom is a bull chasing me through a field. And I have to wait until she gets bored and forgets about me. Or she'll gore out my guts. It could take years."

"Your grandma said that?" my dad asked.

I nodded.

"I'm sure those weren't her exact words," my mother said.

"It's still a very interesting comparison to make with Mrs. Potaski. You know that bulls are male, right?" my dad asked me.

I threw my hands up and accidentally knocked over my glass of milk. "Of course I know that."

My mother brought me a dishrag. "Here you go. And watch the wild arm moves."

I cleaned up the milk while my mom and dad ate their pork chops and peas. I couldn't believe that this conversation made them want to eat. I'd almost lost my entire appetite, because all I wanted to do was improve my life.

After I cleaned up the milk, I put the dishrag in the sink and I stared at my pork chop.

"So which is your favorite class?" my dad asked. "You're taking geology, right?"

I shook my head. "Geography."

"What did you talk about in geography?" he asked.

My mother took a shockingly big bite of her chop.

"Polar stuff," I said.

"About bears?" he asked.

I shook my head again. "Bears are fun and interesting," I said. "We're not studying anything fun or interesting."

"Well, I've got something you can tell your class," my father said. "Ask them if they know why polar bears never eat penguins."

"That's a gross thing to ask a room of strangers," I said.

"She's right," my mother said. "Don't ask them that."

"It's because penguins and polar bears live at opposite ends of the earth. Polar bears live near the North Pole and penguins live near the South Pole."

I did not find that very interesting. "Oh," I said.

"Did you know that bunnies live in polar regions?" my father asked. "Arctic hares. They have a keen sense of smell. I bet we can find some on the Internet after dinner."

"Wouldn't you rather watch TV?" I asked. I knew I would.

And that was what dinner was like. My mom and dad tried to cheer me up and distract me from my Sylvie-less life. And sometimes it worked. But then I would remember that I was Sylvie-less. And it was hard to stay cheered up after I remembered that.

"Bessica," my mother said, after she cleared the table, "don't you want to read Grandma's postcard?"

She handed it to me. On the front was a picture of the four stone faces of Mount Rushmore. Underneath the picture, in big cursive letters, was *Greetings from South Dakota*. I flipped it over. Grandma had written in very clear and small letters:

Bessica!

I miss you so much. Willy and I are enjoying the open road. Did you know that ninety percent of Mount Rushmore was carved by dynamite blasts? The other ten was carved with air hammers. Have you ever seen an air hammer? I have! In case you need to know this for history class, Washington's head was finished in 1930, Jefferson's in 1936, Lincoln's in 1937, and Roosevelt's in 1939. What a rock! Love, your favorite grandma

Bessica Lefter
1556 Beesley Road
Sugar City, Idaho 83448

And then she signed it, *Love, your favorite grandma.*

"Pretty neat postcard," my mom said.

"Yeah," I said. But I would rather have had Grandma in the kitchen. A postcard was just a flat piece of almost nothing. It reminded me of that stupid collaborative diary that Sylvie had tossed into the hole. That was just a bunch of flat pieces of nothing too. Why did people think those things mattered? I put the postcard in the trash.

"Bessica!" my mother said. "You can't throw out your grandma's postcard."

"I just did."

She plucked it out of the trash and frowned at me. "You should save these. Grandma won't be around forever. One day you're going to be glad that you have some mementos."

This was the saddest thing anybody had said to me in a long time. She handed me the card and I took it. And stared at it. And realized that one day Grandma Lefter was going to be as gone as Grandpa Lefter.

"I want Grandma to come home," I said.

"She will," my mom said. "In about six weeks."

I dragged myself to my room and stuck the card next to my bed. Maybe tomorrow would be better, I thought. Maybe Sylvie would call. Maybe all the psycho-bullies would get expelled. Maybe I'd become great friends with Annabelle Deeter's network. Maybe. Maybe. Maybe.

# CHAPTER 13

Sylvie did not call. No psycho-bullies were expelled. And I did not become friends with Annabelle Deeter's network. In nutrition we watched a video about how digestion works, and it made me afraid of my own stomach acid. Then in English the flute music was so loud that I missed some of what Mr. Val was saying.

The smiley dimpled girl in math was absent. And that was a bummer. But I did learn her name, because the teacher called it three times to make sure she wasn't there. "Raya Papas? Raya Papas? Raya Papas?" Then I helped him by saying, "She can't answer you. She's absent." While everyone else around me solved word problems involving sales tax, I decided to solve a different problem. I needed a lunch group. I only knew Annabelle Deeter, Dolan the Puker, three psycho-bullies, the odor girl, and an out-of-control hall monitor. Obviously, I needed to eat lunch with Annabelle and join her network.

On the way to the cafeteria to locate Annabelle, I passed a poster that said the first meeting of the Yearbook Club was happening right then. I stopped in my tracks. This was something I wanted to join. Maybe even more than Annabelle Deeter's network. I had to make a choice: Annabelle Deeter or Yearbook? Unofficial group or official group?

It was a no-brainer. I bought some cookies and headed straight for the Yearbook Club. Annabelle Deeter and her network would also be around tomorrow. But the first meeting of Yearbook Club was happening today.

It started off with the advisor asking the group questions that I thought were weird. "Do you want to document the social interactions of your peers? Are you good at writing snappy captions? Do you naturally think in terms of spatial layout? How many of you feel the graphic novel is an undervalued art form?"

If Sylvie had been there we would have rolled our eyes a lot and made fun of this advisor, because Yearbook shouldn't be lame. Yearbook should be about sneaking around and taking pictures of unsuspecting people looking goofy or coming out of the bathroom. But this advisor couldn't see that. I didn't even write my name down on the sign-up sheet after his lecture. I didn't want to spend another lunch like this, let alone a year. Plus, Cameron Bon Qui Qui was there. And while she might have been a decent hall monitor, she was not a fun person.

After lunch, in geography, we learned about the ideal temperature for penguins to incubate their eggs. We also watched a short film about penguins incubating their eggs, and that was pretty entertaining. But then some of the eggs were duds and no babies hatched and the film ended and I had to go to public speaking. Mrs. Moppett spent most of the class talking about proper posture.

She kept calling kids up to the front and then asking them to exhibit improper posture techniques: slouching, head-forward position, rounded shoulders. Then she would adjust their bodies and demonstrate proper physique. I was terrified that I was going to be called to the front of the class. Thankfully that didn't happen. Redge Marzo had to demonstrate belly breathing versus diaphragmatic breathing. And I took notes, but both of those techniques looked like very weird ways to breathe.

When I got to PE, I had gym clothes with me. My stretch pants were black, not purple. Lots of kids didn't have purple pants, so it wasn't a huge problem. But then Ms. Penrod lectured us a little bit about the importance of proper athletic gear and team spirit:

"Victory starts with impeccable clothes. I could tell you a story about a chance for the world record and a disastrously placed grass stain that would break your hearts.

"I'll give you one week to have the proper attire. Trust me," she said, pointing her toned arm at us, "clothes matter. They can mean the difference between winning and losing." Then she blew her whistle and told us that we needed to run around the gym. Then she blew her whistle again and told us to stop because she'd forgotten to tell us something. I was so tired that I did whatever she said.

"When it comes to physical fitness, variety is the most powerful motivator," she said. "Do you believe me?"

And we all nodded. But I don't think any of us believed her.

"Every Friday we will have a special guest teach us a new fitness skill. Alice Potgeiser has agreed to come in next week and teach us basic and intermediate tumbling."

This was good news. Because I would need some basic and intermediate tumbling skills in order to try out for cheerleading. Now I wouldn't have to find a cable program to learn this stuff. I could just come to PE. When I glanced around, not everybody looked as thrilled as I was about tumbling with Alice Potgeiser. One girl next to me made gagging sounds and said, "Alice is so stuck-up." And the girl next to her said, "Totally."

"Make sure you eat a light lunch that day," Ms. Penrod said. "We'll be tumbling on mats for the entire class."

Then she blew her whistle again and we all started running around the gym. Twenty-seven times. And when I was done and got on the bus, I sort of wanted to drop out of school.

When my mom came home from work, she had some important news. And I immediately thought this news was going to be about me. But it wasn't.

"Foot surgery can really sideline a person," my mom said as she secured plastic wrap over the top of the tuna fish casserole. "I want to go and visit Betty and drop this off, and I want you to come too."

"Why?" I asked. My mom did nice things for people all the time, but I wasn't usually dragged along.

"I need you to hold the casserole." She grabbed her purse.

I thought about objecting in a strenuous way, but I was too tired to do that. Middle school was a real energy zapper. As we drove along, I watched the world fly past me. And I got an idea.

"Can we drive by Sylvie's house?" I asked.

"Isn't she at school?" my mom asked.

"Probably."

"I don't think it's a good idea to stalk her block," my mom said.

But I didn't really have a problem with that. I looked down at the casserole. And I realized that my mom could have set this on the floor or in the backseat and driven to this lady's house without me.

"I understand why you want to give this toe-surgery lady a tuna fish casserole," I said. "But I don't understand why you wanted me to come. You could have put this on the backseat."

"Her name is Betty. Do not call her the toe-surgery lady."

As we drove to Betty's house, I got curious as to what exactly had been wrong with her toes.

"Was it fungus?" I asked. That was probably a serious and common toe problem for the elderly.

"It wasn't fungus. It was structural. She suffered from severe mallet toe."

The casserole didn't stink like fish at all. It smelled like cheese and bacon. I lifted the plastic wrap off of a corner of the dish so the smell could escape more easily. I really liked that smell. It reminded me of pizza. Sort of.

"Do you know what mallet toe is?" my mother asked.

"A terrible deformity that makes it impossible to wear sandals?"

My mother stopped at a red light and frowned at me. "You shouldn't make fun of people with toe deformities."

"I was being serious," I said.

"Mallet toe is a condition where a toe curls due to a bend in the top of the toe joint."

"Did the doctor have to break her toe to fix it?" I asked.

"Not quite," she said. "Do you really want to hear the details? Her toe was quite rigid, so fixing it required some invasive action."

"I'll use my imagination," I said.

When we pulled up to Betty's house, I noticed a brown dog out front. It looked small, but I could see its teeth. "Will that dog attack me if I'm carrying a casserole that has a bacon scent?" I asked.

"Let me carry the casserole," my mom said.

So we walked up Betty's driveway and the toothy brown dog didn't bother us at all. In fact, it ran around to the backyard like a total coward. We got to the front door and my mom didn't even knock. She pushed Betty's big red door right open. And that surprised me. So I tugged on my mom's shirt a little bit in disapproval.

"We're breaking into her house?" I asked.

"She knows I'm coming and she's bedridden," my mom said.

Once we were inside mallet-toe Betty's house, I realized that she was a weird person. Because in addition to having almost no furniture, and a bicycle in her living room, Betty had otters everywhere. She had photos of them. And pillows of them. And statues of them. And paintings of them. They hung all over her aqua blue walls and lined her dusty windowsills. Betty even had macaroni art that looked like fat, splashing otters hanging in her dining room.

"What's with the otters?" I asked. "And where is her couch?"

But my mom didn't answer. "Betty?" she called. "Betty?"

"I'm in the bedroom," a voice answered.

I stopped. It felt weird to walk into a stranger's bedroom. "I'll wait here," I said. "By the bike."

But my mom set the casserole down on the kitchen counter and shepherded me into Betty's bedroom.

I was relieved to see that Betty had a bed, but I was alarmed by how terrible she looked. Her hair was greasy and gray. And she didn't have any makeup on. She wore a blue bathrobe and her skin glowed a very pale color and I could see her blue leg veins. One of her feet was bandaged and elevated on a pillow. Her television hung from the ceiling like TVs do in hospital rooms. She was watching a show about otters.

"It's so good to see you, Bambi," Betty said.

My mom's name was Bambi.

"We brought you a casserole," my mom said. "We'll leave it in the fridge."

"Oh!" Betty squealed. "That is so sweet. All I've eaten since the surgery is frozen burritos."

When I heard this I frowned. And I quit breathing deeply, because I realized that I smelled burritos, and that was not a pleasant odor.

"Do you need help with anything? Laundry? Yard work?" my mom asked.

I kept looking around Betty's bedroom. She had a ton of pictures on her blue walls. They were of people who looked like Betty who were doing vacation things. Swimming. Boating. Riding donkeys.

"It's nice just to have somebody to talk to," Betty said.

Which was an awful thing for Betty to say, because that meant we had to stay longer and have a conversation with her. My mom sat down on a footstool and I stood next to her.

"Are you Bessica?" Betty asked. "Your mother has told me so much about you."

"Cool," I said.

"Bessica just had her first week of middle school," my mom said.

"Oh," Betty moaned. "Middle school. I'm glad I'm done with that."

"Did you have terrible teachers?" I asked. My mind flashed to PE and Ms. Penrod.

Betty shook her head. "Middle school is a cruel institution. The food is terrible. The lessons are often meaningless. And the students are little demons. If you can survive that, you can survive anything."

And while Betty was talking, I heard something besides Betty. It was a squeaky sound. And it was coming from outside. When I looked out the window, I saw somebody I knew bouncing into the air. It was the dimpled girl who'd been absent from math class. Raya Papas. And she was jumping on a trampoline next door.

"Demons!" Betty said.

This made me take a small step back, because if I followed Betty's logic, she was telling me that I was a demon.

"Bessica finds middle school exciting," my mom said.

"No, I don't," I said. "I find it puke-bad."

"And it only gets worse," Betty said.

"Now, Betty," my mom said. "Let's not be too negative."

I stopped watching Raya bounce and started watching Betty. She was turning a pink color.

"It's pure and total horror," Betty said. She sat straight up and wagged her finger at me. "I'd rather have surgery on all ten of my toes than go back and face one day of middle school." Then she leaned back down and her pillows made a plopping sound.

"Wow," I said. Usually adults weren't this honest. I looked around the room and noticed an orange prescription bottle on the floor. "Are you taking painkillers?" I asked. Grandma took those once and she became very talkative and direct during that time. Betty ignored my question.

"Are you being forced to take public speaking?" Betty asked.

"I am," I said.

"Let's stay positive," my mother interjected.

"Know this," Betty said. "You can't win. Say what they want you to say. Do whatever they tell you to do. Keep your head down. Avoid everyone."

While Betty was talking, I heard a panicked scream from next door and I saw Raya Papas fly off the trampoline. Then I heard a thud. And that was followed by moaning. This made me gasp a little, because it was like mallet-toe Betty and my mom didn't know that Raya Papas might have just gotten killed. I was the only one who knew that.

"Hey," I said. But my mom interrupted me.

"Betty, Bessica likes her public speaking teacher."

"No, I don't," I said.

"The institution," Betty said. "It wants to flatten you. Don't join their clubs. Don't eat their food. Don't play with the demons. Tell the world to leave you alone and it will."

"Okay," I said.

But really, I thought that mallet-toe Betty might be

crazy, and I was hoping we could get out of there and possibly check on Raya.

"You think I'm joking," Betty said. "And I'm not. The institution is a system. It will turn you into a potato."

But then Betty started snoring.

"She's tired and medicated," my mother said. "She didn't mean any of it."

"I think she did," I said. I'd never thought of middle school as an institution or a system. "Middle school wants to turn me into a potato."

It sounded totally crazy, but not any crazier than psycho-bullies or Dolan the Puker.

"That doesn't make any sense, Bessica," my mother said.

But it did. Mallet-toe Betty made a lot of weird sense. And as we left her house, I told my mom that I wanted to go check on Raya.

"I saw her fly off the trampoline," I said. "And that was followed by moaning."

"Why didn't you say something?" my mother asked.

"Betty was talking," I said.

When we got into Raya's backyard, there wasn't anything but a trampoline and a pair of shoes.

"These are just like my shoes!" I said, picking one up. Then I looked to see what color tongues she'd attached, and they were yellow. I hadn't used my yellow tongues yet.

"Do you want to knock?" my mom asked.

I looked around her yard and it seemed empty. Her house seemed empty too. I figured either Raya was in a hospital dying or already dead, or she was sleeping, and I should probably wait to see her again in school. Because it wasn't like she was my friend. She was just a person with dimples who sat next to me in math and ignored me.

"I'm ready to go home," I said, putting the shoe down.

As we rode along, even though my mom had said that she thought it was a bad idea to stalk Sylvie's block, she drove past her house. But I didn't see anybody. Her house sat in her yard and looked like an empty shell. And I watched that empty shell until it faded away.

# CHAPTER 14

**E**ven though Yearbook hadn't turned out so hot, I hadn't given up on becoming an official member of something. That week there were a lot of lunch meetings with a variety of clubs: chorus and math among them. I liked the idea of buying vending-machine cookies and eating them during these lunch meetings. And cheerleading try-outs were coming up too. They happened after school. And I couldn't help thinking that if I made the squad, I wouldn't have to worry about finding a lunch group. I'd have an automatic one.

I waited for the bus in my driveway. The sun wasn't up yet. In fact, I could still see the moon and the North Star.

I stood beside the road, wearing my cute red jacket and matching red sneaker tongues. The cold morning air made me shiver a little bit. Even though fall had just begun, I was going to need to start wearing my winter coat. It was a bummer, because I liked my cute red jacket more than my blue puffer coat. I looked back at my humming porch light. No other lights in my house were on. My mom had probably gone back to bed.

I waited and waited. Then, even though I knew I shouldn't abandon the bus line, I decided to go check on something important. I set down my backpack and crossed my yard to get to my neighbor's yard. Noll Beck was still sleeping, so it seemed like a good time to spy on the Mustang.

I knew Noll would never be my boyfriend, since I was eleven and he was fifteen. As Grandma had pointed out several times, those were four very important years. But I couldn't keep myself from daydreaming about him. Noll was tall, so I could see his gorgeous head popping up over our redwood fence when he played basketball.

He drove around in his shiny green Mustang, and when Noll saw me, he always asked me the same wonderful question, "Hey, Messica, what's new on the menu?" And while Sylvie thought Noll was teasing me in an unkind way when he called me Messica and asked me about menu items, I knew that Noll Beck wasn't being mean at all. He was flirting with me. Because boys weren't smart like girls. And so instead of saying smart, kind flirty things, they said dumb, weird flirty things. And this didn't bother me at all. Because I really liked it when Noll Beck talked to me, no matter what he said.

When I got to the Mustang, I was bummed out right away, because other than some crumpled papers, it was basically empty. Normally, it had interesting stuff in it. And Sylvie and I would make a mental inventory and then go back to my bedroom and figure out what kind of person Noll was and what he did in his free time. Once, we'd seen a birthday cake for Noll and it was shaped like a football. So I knew that football was his favorite sport. And I repeatedly saw a chemistry book in there, so I knew that Noll must be brilliant. And I saw a bag of dog food in there once, so I knew that Noll liked animals. And one time there was a box of paint cans, so I knew that Noll liked color.

Sylvie would sometimes bring up that we didn't know for sure what was Noll's stuff versus other random people's who he gave rides to. But I could tell. Noll's stuff was cool and interesting. And other random people's stuff was mainly the garbage in the car. One time I saw that the car was unlocked, and so I opened the door, but Sylvie got very upset and said that she didn't want to violate anybody's privacy. But I saw it differently. Getting in the car would teach me a lot about Noll, because if he was a maniac, it was my duty to find out.

That morning, as I waited for the bus, I stared at the backseat, trying to figure out what the crumpled papers were all about. Were they garbage? Were they break-up letters from a girl he was dating? Why would any girl want to break up with Noll Beck? My mind was working so hard that I forgot that I was on my way to school. Then I heard the bus and remembered.

I bolted through the Becks' front yard and through my front yard, and made it to the driveway right as the bus started flashing its lights. I scooped up my backpack and raced across the road before the bus driver even flipped out the Stop sign. I ran up the stairs.

"You look so eager!" the bus driver said.

But I didn't say anything back. I didn't even look at him. Because conversing with the bus driver was a surefire way to become less popular than I already was.

My bus wasn't all that crowded, so I usually sat by myself. I didn't mind that too much. It was better than sitting next to a weirdo. And, sadly, there were a few of those on my bus. I held my backpack close and thought about all the people I didn't want to encounter that day. There were a lot. Maybe mallet-toe Betty was right. When it came to middle school, the kids were demons. Except me. I was normal.

When the bus squeaked to a stop in front of the school, I felt my stomach tighten. Getting off the bus had become a risky activity for me, because I never knew whether I was going to bump into one of the psycho-bullies. And they always teased me by asking the same question: "Are you going to walk, or are you going to run?" And I usually just ignored them and kept walking. Jerks. I didn't even understand why psycho-bully Redge came to school. I mean, how did anyone expect to learn anything without a pen?

I hurried into school and went to my locker. My combination was still hard for me to remember. Sylvie had gotten 2, 5, 10. Which was a basic math problem. I'd gotten 40, 6, 23. Which wasn't any math problem. It was just a bunch of numbers with no relevance that were challenging to remember. Once I opened my locker, I realized that I didn't need anything, so I slammed it shut. Then I felt somebody breathing on me. Her breath smelled like pancakes. I turned around.

"You didn't stay for Yearbook Club," Cameron Bon Qui Qui said.

"Yes I did," I said. "I just never went back."

Cameron Bon Qui Qui smiled at me. "I've been chosen to be the lead photographer."

"Oh," I said. Then I felt even better about my decision not to join.

"Don't think you can miss the first month and then show up once we start taking pictures or designing the layout."

"Okay," I said.

"Sometimes slackers think they can skip the hard stuff and then show up for the party."

"I'm not a slacker," I said. "But I usually like parties."

Cameron Bon Qui Qui narrowed her eyes. "You know what I mean."

I nodded. A couple of weeks ago, my hair would have flown around my shoulders when I nodded. But my pixie cut didn't move at all.

"I just hung up more posters." She pointed to one so I could see it. It was about a Going Green Club that was meeting in the gym on Friday after school. And there were a bunch about our school vote for mascot next week. There were a lot of pictures of wolves and bears. "If you take any down, I will report you. I know your name now, Bessica."

And when she said this, she blew her pancake breath on me a little bit and it sort of felt like I was being threatened by the hall monitor. And I would have preferred not to feel that way.

"Don't worry. I already know what animal mascot I'm voting for. And I'm not going to the Going Green Club," I said. "I'll be attending cheerleader tryouts."

And then Cameron Bon Qui Qui held back laughter and walked off.

As I walked to my next class, I passed a bunch of familiar-looking faces. Some of them seemed friendly. But I didn't know their names. And even if I did, I didn't know what to say. They looked so comfortable walking down the halls. They looked like they knew where they belonged. I wanted to look like that too.

When I took my seat in Mrs. Mounds's class, I grabbed a pen out of my pen case and handed it to psycho-bully Redge. He didn't say thank you.

"Do you have one with blue ink?" he asked. "Blue is my favorite color."

The bell rang.

I dug through my pen case until I found one with blue ink. I handed it to him, but he didn't give my first pen back.

I held my hand out. He slapped it like he was giving me five.

"I want my other pen back," I said.

"I want waffles," he said. Then he growled at me and I turned back around.

"Today we are going to talk about the importance of sugar and the brain," Mrs. Mounds said. She wrote something on the board in pink letters. Then she started drawing a pink glob of something.

"What's that?" a student in the front of the class asked.

"This is a picture of your brain," Mrs. Mounds said.

It looked like a gigantic walnut. And as I stared at that walnut, all I could think about was my pen. I turned around.

"Okay, you can keep two pens this time," I told him. "But this means you don't get a pen tomorrow."

"Who's talking?" Mrs. Mounds asked. She turned around and showed us her pinched, angry face. "It's disrespectful to talk when I'm working at the board."

"It was somebody in the back," a student in the middle of the class said. "It sounded like Bessica Lefter."

I sat straight up. How did anybody know what I sounded like?

Mrs. Mounds looked straight at me. And I knew what was going to happen next. I knew Mrs. Mounds was going to ask me if I'd been talking. And I was going to have to be honest and say yes. Then she would write my name down in brown marker. And I would lose more valuable points. And I would get further and further behind. I took a deep breath. Why did middle school have to be so terrible?

But none of that happened.

Mrs. Mounds cleared her throat. "Let's focus on the brain." Then she kept writing. "I plan on saying some enlightening things."

I felt so relieved. I thought I was going to have another rotten day. But then it looked like I wasn't. Because something good had happened to me when I didn't even expect it to, and I'd only been at school for fifteen minutes. At this rate, probably twenty more good things would happen to me by lunch. I took out a pen and wrote down everything Mrs. Mounds said about the brain.

"Your brain is about the size of a cantaloupe."

"Your brain uses less power than a refrigerator light."

"In one day your brain generates more electrical impulses than all the telephones in the world."

Also, Mrs. Mounds went off track and mentioned interesting things that didn't have anything to do with the brain. But I wrote those down too.

# CHAPTER 15

When you are in middle school, it is a dumb idea to expect good things to happen to you. After nutrition I had English. And nothing good happened in there. And after English I had math. And maybe something good happened, but I can't remember. Because I fell asleep. And when I woke up, class was pretty much over and we'd apparently discussed a formula that calculates all the fat parts of a circle.

At one point, I thought something good had happened. Because Raya Papas came in while I was sleeping. When class started, I noticed that her chair was empty. When I woke from napping, Raya was in her seat. She didn't look like she'd broken her neck at all. She was very involved writing a note and putting heart stickers on it. And I thought that I would like to get a note with a heart sticker on it from Raya. Did she even know my name? I reached over and touched her shoulder.

"What do you want?" Raya asked.

She didn't sound as friendly as she looked.

"I like your stickers," I said.

"Why are you spying on me?" She slid her note under her spiral notebook.

I wasn't quite sure what to say. So I skipped to a new topic. "Hey. Where do you live?" Because I wanted to tell Raya that I'd seen her fall off that trampoline.

Raya wrinkled her face. "Why? Do you want to come spy on me at my house?"

I shook my head. Because I'd already done that. "I was just curious."

Raya turned and faced the girl on the other side of her. I watched her hand the note to her. Then she faced the front of the room. And she never told me where she lived. Which made it hard for me to bring up her trampoline. So I didn't. Raya Papas was treating me like a potential kidnapper, and nobody had ever done that to me before.

As my boring teacher wrapped up his boring discussion about how to determine the surface area of a cube, it was pretty clear that I would not be eating lunch with Raya Papas. This became especially clear when the bell rang and we filed out of class and I timed things so that I could leave class with Raya.

"Do you sleep in all your classes?" Raya asked me.

"No," I said. "Just math."

"You talk in your sleep," Raya said.

I tried to stop my face from making a freaked-out expression.

"Do I say interesting things?" I asked.

"No," Raya said. "You kept saying one word over and over and over."

And I wasn't sure that I wanted to know what this word was, but Raya told me anyway.

"Potato." Raya walked into the hallway. "You repeated it in a moaning way. You must be starving."

And I was a little bit excited when Raya said that, because if she thought I was starving, maybe she'd suggest eating with me. But she didn't.

"You made it really hard to focus," Raya said. "If it happens again, I'm going to ask to move my seat." Then Raya walked off in her supercute clothes with her supercute friend.

I didn't even bother going to the cafeteria. I headed to the vending machine and the alt crowd. Because there weren't any club meetings to attend today. I was starting to feel that the hallway and the alt crowd were right where I belonged.

As I stood in front of the vending machine, I could see my own bummed-out reflection in the glass. I pulled a dollar bill out and fed it into the machine. Then I pushed the button for oatmeal raisin cookies. But something rotten happened. The bag got caught on the metal spiral dispenser. I pushed the button again, but nothing happened.

"Hurry up," some boy said behind me.

But I couldn't hurry. Because my purchase wouldn't drop.

"My cookies are stuck," I said, pushing the button rapidly.

"Buy something else," the boy said.

"But I already paid," I said.

"That's not our problem," the boy said.

I turned around to see who was being so rude in the vending-machine line. And I wasn't too surprised when I saw it was psycho-bully Cola. I turned back around and pressed the button again.

"Hurry up!" psycho-bully Cola said. "Lunch is only thirty minutes."

"I know!" But then I just stood there and looked at my cookies. I stared at them really hard, trying to make them fall. But they didn't.

Then I felt somebody standing next to me. At first I thought it was Cola. But the person was much taller than Cola. Then I thought maybe it was a teacher. But the person was wearing boots with black electrical tape wrapped around them. So I looked at the person. And I swallowed hard. She was very alt. She had black clothes, black hair, black lipstick, and black nail polish, and she was wearing what looked like a black studded dog collar. Also, most of her head was shaved. All except a thick line in the middle.

"My cookies are stuck," I explained.

She frowned at the machine. "You have to kick it."

I shook my head. Because I didn't want to attack the machine.

"Fine," she said. "I'll kick it."

And the girl kicked the side of the vending machine with her big black boots. *Bam. Bam. Bam.* "Drop!" she yelled.

But my cookies didn't drop.

She kicked again. And again. Harder. It sounded like somebody was hitting a trash can with a baseball bat. *Slam! Slam! Slam!*

And then my cookies finally fell.

"Thanks!" I said.

But the alt girl wasn't finished. I think she was a very angry person, because she kicked the vending machine very powerfully one more time. *Kaboom!* And this time, instead of smashing her boot against the machine's side, her heel made contact with the glass front. And I heard an awful sound. It was the sound of glass cracking.

"Holy crud!" I yelled. "You broke the glass!"

"Didn't mean to," the alt girl said.

Then, out of nowhere, a teacher I didn't know showed up. She was wearing ugly brown pants. And a whistle.

"Who did this?" the teacher asked.

And psycho-bully Cola jumped in right away with the answer. "Bessica Lefter and Nadia Strom! I saw them."

And I didn't even have a chance to point out that I hadn't attacked the machine like Nadia; I'd only attempted to buy a zero-nutrition lunch.

"Bessica and Nadia," the teacher said. "Come with me!"

I tried to reach into the vending machine and get my cookies, but the teacher wouldn't let me.

"Stop touching the machine!" the teacher said.

"I just wanted my cookies," I mumbled.

And so we followed the teacher to the principal's office. I was too scared to cry. I felt pretty terrible. Because it didn't seem fair that I was going to have to miss my lunch and leave my cookies in the vending machine for somebody else (probably psycho-bully Cola) to eat. But that was exactly what was happening.

When we got to the principal's office, the teacher told us to sit down. Then she went inside to talk to the principal.

I looked at Nadia. She was digging through her black furry bag for something.

"Is that made out of a bear?" I asked. Because I couldn't think of another black furry animal.

Nadia frowned at me. "It's fake," she said. "I'm not a murderer."

"Oh," I said. "I don't have a bag. I just have a backpack. It's in my locker."

Then Nadia and I sat there in silence. The clock on the wall ticked and ticked.

"Will they call my mom?" I asked.

"Yeah," Nadia said. "They've probably already done that."

"Are we going to be billed for the damage to the machine?" I asked. I had no idea how much the front of a vending machine would cost.

"You won't," she said. "You didn't kick it."

It was encouraging to hear Nadia taking the full blame for the incident. Because really, me and my cookies were just innocent bystanders.

"Am I going to get suspended?" I asked.

Nadia looked at me. She had such an intense stare. Like if she turned her gaze toward a raw steak, she'd be able to cook it.

"Officially, nothing is going to happen to you," she said. "You didn't do anything."

"Cool," I said. And I thought maybe I should offer to

take a teeny bit of the blame for Nadia. But I worried that if I did, my parents might freak out. Also, I worried that if Mrs. Potaski ever heard about this incident, I would need to look as innocent as possible. And that meant not taking any blame.

I smiled at Nadia. "You're right. I didn't do anything."

Then Nadia said something troubling.

"Unofficially, you're probably going to be socially certified as hard-core alt."

I didn't quite know what that meant. "You mean I'll be expected to hang out with the other hard-core alt kids?" I asked. And I liked that idea a little bit. Because at least I'd be part of something, even if it was unofficial and antisocial.

"No," she said. "The hard-core alt kids don't hang out with anybody. They spend all their time in loner town, like me. And, in light of the day's events, most likely you too."

"What?" I asked. How was I supposed to make friends in loner town? "But I want to join chorus. And maybe become a cheerleader."

"That's too bad," Nadia said. "Once you end up in loner town, you never get out."

My mind flashed to a commercial about bug traps for killing roaches. "That's impossible," I said. "Somebody has to have gotten out of loner town before."

Nadia tapped her finger on her chair leg. "Nobody. Never."

I felt very panicked. Because I did not want to spend three years in middle school living in loner town without any friends. Who would want that?

"There must be something I can do," I said.

"Switch schools," Nadia said. "That's your only option."

"No. There's got to be a solution." Grandma once said that there was a solution to everything. Even bloodstains on a white carpet. You just had to think creatively.

"Listen," Nadia said. "You'll like loner town. Cookies every day."

This made me frown a little bit. Because I did not think that cookies were more important than friends. My mind spun as I considered my new, terrible reputation. Then I thought of something Marci and Vicki had told me.

"How close is loner town to the row?" I asked. I was hoping they were at opposite ends of the school.

Nadia almost laughed. "Loner town *is* the row."

My eyes grew very wide and I mouthed the word *no*.

This could not be happening. I could not spend the next three years eating lunch in a hallway with criminals and malfunctioning lightbulbs. I breathed very quickly and looked around the principal's office. I needed a solution very badly. And then it hit me. It was the most obvious solution in the world. If I became a cheerleader, I would become automatic friends with all the other cheerleaders and there was no way I'd end up in loner town.

"All I have to do is become a cheerleader," I said. "That will solve everything."

Nadia scowled. "That's lame. And highly improbable."

I sat up straighter. "No, it's not. All it takes is the power of visualization."

And before I could explain to Nadia about how the power of visualization worked, Principal Tidge came out. Until this moment, I had only seen Principal Tidge from long distances. Up close, she looked pretty cute. Except she was a terrible dresser. She had a nice, round face; a small, round nose; bright green eyes; and a long neck. But her clothes were rotten. She was dressed in all gray. Gray sweater. Gray pants. Gray shoes. She had a red shirt on underneath all the gray that poked out a little bit, but not enough. And she wore a big gold pin that looked like a fish. She smelled like deodorant.

"I'm very disappointed that you two girls decided to vandalize the vending machine," she said. "We've called your parents. Nadia, considering your offenses last year, this will result in suspension."

"That's cool," Nadia said.

"Bessica," the principal said.

And when I heard the principal say my name, my throat

grew tight and tears started slipping out of my eyes. And I decided I needed to explain myself.

"But I didn't do anything!" I said. "I paid for cookies and they didn't drop. And then Cola kept yelling at me to hurry. And so I pushed the buttons again. *Gently*. And then Nadia showed up and attacked the vending machine."

"Are you sure that's an accurate depiction of events?" the principal asked. "You didn't touch the vending machine in any way?"

I reached my hands out toward the principal in a pleading way. "Just to make my selection. *Gently*."

The principal rubbed her temples. It looked like this situation was giving her a headache. "Is this true?" she asked Nadia.

"Pretty much," Nadia said.

"Bessica, return to lunch. We'll call your mother and tell her it was a misunderstanding."

But I really wanted the principal to be able to erase the whole event so I didn't end up in loner town.

"You mean she doesn't get a refund?" Nadia asked. "She never got her cookies."

It was too bad that Nadia was a hard-core alt person who wore a dog collar and got suspended and lived in loner town, because thus far she was the nicest person I'd met in middle school.

"That's true," I said. "I was told to leave my cookies in the machine."

The principal rubbed her temples again. "Wait here. I'll have Mrs. Batts get you a refund. Nadia, go to my office."

And even though Nadia didn't see me give her a friendly wave goodbye, I did. Then I sat back down and waited for my refund.

"Bessica Lefter," Mrs. Batts said. "Wait right here and I'll be back with your change."

As she walked away, I looked at my legs and wondered how long it would take them to learn to do the splits all the way. I kicked them a little. I figured a week. And if I practiced cheerleading bending at home, and paid total attention in PE during basic and intermediate tumbling, and visualized, visualized, visualized, this could work! I sat back in my chair, feeling very relieved. For about three seconds. And then a girl with an enormous fluffy ponytail came in and said something to me that was so terrible that I wanted a mountain lion to show up and eat me whole.

"Bessica Lefter?" the girl with the puffy ponytail said.

She must have heard Mrs. Batts call me by my name. I didn't answer her.

Then she smiled so big that I could see her top and bottom teeth. "I've heard about you. You like Kettle Harris? I know. I read all about it."

I didn't say anything. I couldn't. It was like somebody

had dropped a bomb on me. I'd barely figured out how to escape dangerous/deadly loner town and become a cheerleader, and now this. The diary. Sylvie. I couldn't believe it! She showed it to people. Before we threw it away, or maybe when she kept the pages.

The fluffy-headed girl kept smiling as she flitted through the office. I felt myself turning several shades of angry red. Stupid diary. Stupid Sylvie. Why had she kept the pages that talked about me liking Kettle Harris? What was wrong with her? I hadn't shown that to anybody. I was smart enough to know that was a terrible idea. And how did Sylvie even know the puffy-headed girl? Were they secret friends? And who else had Sylvie shown that stupid diary to?

And then that puffy-headed girl took the attendance slips and left before I could deny what she'd said. And when Mrs. Batts came in and handed me my refund, it didn't feel as great as it should have. The bell rang and lunch was over.

"I'm going to write a note giving you permission to eat in class," Mrs. Batts said.

"Thanks," I said. But it was hard for me to think about lunch and cookies. I didn't know one lunch could be this bad. First I found out that I had to become a cheerleader or I'd be socially certified as "nothing" in a deadly area for three years. Then I found out that Sylvie was a total jerk. It sure was a good thing that Sylvie and I weren't friends anymore. Because if we were, I would have called her up and yelled at her and told her how rotten she was. Then, as I walked to my stupid geography class, I realized I could call Sylvie up and yell at her and tell her how rotten she was, even though we weren't friends anymore. In fact, if I didn't do that, Sylvie would never know that I knew she was rotten. And I couldn't let that happen.

I decided that I'd call her that night. I'd call her right up and ask her what her problem was. And if she pretended that she didn't know what I was talking about, then I'd just yell more. And say superterrible things. Because she deserved that. She totally did.

# CHAPTER 16

Traditionally, Monday was the day that my grandmother was in charge of dinner. She wasn't expected to do this. But she was the sort of person who liked to contribute. Grandma used to set the table, turn off both televisions, light candles, and serve dinner. She didn't like to cook meals from scratch. Just dessert. So for dinner she brought home corn dogs from the Corny Spot. And I guess I thought my family would keep this tradition alive in honor of Grandma. But I was wrong. Because that tradition died pretty quickly.

My mother thought making fake meat loaf would be a

nice change of pace. But her fake meat loaf wasn't so hot. Instead of meat, she made it with ricotta cheese and brown rice and a large number of spices that we normally never ate. In fact, it tasted so terrible that my dad and I were forced to use a variety of condiments to disguise the fake taste.

"Try more ketchup," my mom suggested.

My dad pounded the butt of the bottle a few more times.

"It tastes like I'm eating a shoe," he said.

In addition to tasting bad, it was also gray. And I didn't find gray food appealing. Also, now I associated it with my principal.

"I miss corn dogs," my father said.

I nodded.

"Do you know what's in a corn dog?" my mother asked.

"A hot dog?" I answered.

"And do you know what's in a hot dog?" my mother asked.

"Meat fat and filler?" I said.

My mother's eyes widened. She was surprised that I knew what was inside a hot dog. "And possibly carcinogenic nitrite additives."

"Let's not say that word at the dinner table," my father said.

But I wasn't totally sure what *carcinogenic* meant. And in

my family, if you didn't know what a word meant, it was totally acceptable to interrupt the conversation and ask for the word to be defined.

"Please define *carcinogenic*," I said.

My father glanced at my mother. She set her fork down.

"*Carcinogenic* means that it can cause cancer," my mother said.

And then I set my fork down too. "Grandma fed us carcinogenic corn dogs for five years and you let her?" I asked. I knew it was polite to be nice to old people, but this was ridiculous.

"Just because you eat a hot dog doesn't mean you'll get cancer," my dad said.

"And some of them don't have nitrite additives. Like you said, some are just meat fat and filler," my mom said.

I shook my head. And then I stared at my plate. "Have I ever eaten a carcinogenic hot dog?" I asked.

My parents looked at each other again. But they didn't say anything.

"I have eaten a carcinogenic hot dog, haven't I?" I asked. I was disgusted to learn this.

"You're overreacting," my father said.

"Yes," my mother said. "Calm down."

But I wasn't overreacting. Grandpa Lefter had died of cancer ten years ago. That meant cancer could happen to other people in my family. Like me.

"Let's just eat our meat loaf," my mother said. "The center is better than the edges."

I stared at the center of my fake meat loaf. It was very, very gray.

"Your homework pile looks huge tonight," my dad said.

"It was that big Friday night," I said. "I have a feeling it's always going to be that big. Maybe bigger." I poked my meat loaf again. I guess I sort of expected it to react.

"How was geography?" my dad asked. "Are you studying bears yet?"

I shook my head.

"What did you learn?" he asked.

I thought very hard. I didn't take a lot of notes in geography today, on account of the fact that I was completely freaked out about living in loner town and people having read my diary. Also, I was eating my lunch cookies. "I learned that some days in the Arctic during the winter, the sun never rises and during the summer, the sun never sets."

My dad whistled. Which is something he did when he heard an interesting fact or statistic. Then he stabbed his meat loaf again. "I need more ketchup."

I passed him the bottle. It was almost empty. *Whap. Whap. Whap.*

Then there was a lot of silence while we chewed. And I wasn't sure what we should talk about. I was a little distracted, because I kept playing the conversation that I wanted to have with Sylvie in my head.

*"When you showed people our diary, did they have to come to your house or did you let them take it home? Did anybody photocopy it? Why do you want to destroy my life, Sylvie? And when did you become such an awful person?"*

Then my dad asked me another question, and I stopped thinking about how miserable I was over what Sylvie had done and started thinking about how miserably things had gone for me at lunch today.

"You'll never guess who I bumped into at my last stop," my dad said. "Principal Tidge's husband."

I swallowed hard and looked at my mom.

"What?" my dad asked. "Why are you both making that face? You don't like Mr. Tidge?"

Then my mom started talking, and I felt pretty bummed out, because it was obvious that she was going to tell him all about the vending-machine incident.

"I should probably tell you that the principal's office called today to notify me that Bessica was involved in a vending-machine incident."

My father took a big swallow of milk.

"Did the machine rip you off?" my dad asked. "Sometimes they do that. If that happens, you need to go to the secretary and ask for a refund."

"Oh, I got my refund," I said.

"Aren't you concerned that our daughter is eating out of the vending machines?" my mother asked. "Talk about carcinogenic additives. Those things shouldn't even be allowed in schools."

"Maybe Bessica was eating something nutritious," my dad said. "Like an organic granola bar. Or an apple."

He looked at me.

"I purchased oatmeal-raisin cookies," I said. "Sugar is the second ingredient."

My father sighed. "Tell me about the vending-machine incident."

"At first, the principal told me that Bessica had vandalized the machine and broken the glass," my mother said.

My father's eyes got big. "What?"

"But then the principal called again because another girl admitted that Bessica hadn't done any such thing," my mom said.

"A girl broke the glass?" my dad asked. "Did she use a heavy object?"

I nodded. "Her boot. She kicked it seven times. My cookies wouldn't drop."

"And what did you do?" my father asked.

I shrugged. "I waited for my cookies to drop."

My father did not look pleased with this answer.

"You didn't get a teacher?" he asked.

"That's not always the best answer," I said.

"Everything sorted itself out," my mother said.

"Sounds like North Teton Middle School has a tough crowd," my dad said.

"Nadia is totally tough."

"Nadia sounds like trouble," my dad said.

"Yeah," I said. "But she's suspended. Also, she wears a dog collar and she spends all her time in loner town. We're not friends." And I didn't bother going into how I didn't have any other friends yet, and would be stuck in loner town for three years unless I became a cheerleader.

"The school system has changed a lot since I was a sixth grader," he said.

"I know," my mother said. "The PE teacher at Bessica's school is a former Olympian. She threw the shot put."

My dad whistled again.

"How did you know that?" I asked.

"Your schedule is on the refrigerator," my mom said.

"But how did you know Ms. Penrod is a former Olympian? Is she famous?" I liked the idea of having a famous teacher. Even if she was determined to kick my butt.

"There was an article about her in the paper. Do you want to read it?" she asked.

"No," I said.

"Has she had you throw the shot yet?" my dad asked. "It can weigh as much as sixteen pounds."

I shook my head. "I haven't even seen a shot. We jog a lot. It's her favorite. Also, for variety, we're learning basic and intermediate tumbling tomorrow."

My dad looked thrilled. "Variety," he said. "It's the spice of life."

"Whatever," I said. "I'm finished." Even though I still had a lot of loaf left.

"Should we go for a walk?" asked my mom.

On Mondays, after dinner, we used to walk with Grandma around our block so we could monitor hedgehog destruction. I looked at Grandma's empty chair. It was a very sad-looking empty chair. She'd left her cushion on it. I wondered if she knew she'd left that.

"No," I said. "I've got things to do." I wondered if it made sense to write a letter to Kettle, even though I didn't know where he lived, and deny that I'd ever liked him. Maybe I should send a copy of this letter to the fluffy-haired girl. When it came to my new problem, I wasn't sure of the best solution.

"If you need any help with your homework, just ask," my dad said.

"I will," I said. Even though the truth was I planned to attempt to do splits and then call Sylvie and yell at her.

And none of that was really a school assignment. I could do my homework after that. And maybe do more cheer-leader bending.

I went to my room and waited for Sylvie to get home from school. She had no idea what she had coming.

# CHAPTER

Maybe Sylvie did have an idea of what she had coming, because I called her three times and she never answered her phone. I bet my name came up on her caller ID. That was when I realized that she was probably screening her phone calls and that I needed to come up with a better plan.

But before I could do that, my mom knocked on my bedroom door.

"What?" I said. "I'm busy." I wasn't trying to sound rude, but it was important that my mother understood that I wasn't always available to talk to her when she knocked.

"Your backpack is in the living room," my mom said. "Didn't you say you had homework?"

"Yeah," I said. "I need that."

When my mom opened my door and brought me my backpack, she looked worried. "Why are you just sitting in here on the floor with your phone?"

She sat down next to me and put her arm around me. "I want you to know that you can tell me anything."

"Okay," I said.

My mother rubbed my back. "It's about Nadia, isn't it? Sometimes older and insecure kids don't treat people the way they should," my mom said. "They take out their frustrations on other people."

"That's true," I said. But I had no idea where my mom was going with this.

"I need you to tell me the truth, Bessica." She sighed very heavily and rubbed my back more. "Is Nadia bullying you? Because if she is, I need to report her."

I shook my head. "What are you talking about?"

"The way you described her makes her sound very intimidating. I imagine you might be afraid to speak up about her. But Bessica, if you're in danger, you should speak up now."

I couldn't believe that my mother was insane. I'd thought it was just Sylvie's mother who had mental problems. "I'm not in danger. I don't even know Nadia."

My mother stopped rubbing my back and started picking up my dirty socks. There were a lot of them. "So you just happened to run into her at the vending machine and she kicked the tar out of the machine for no reason?"

"Pretty much," I said. "That's what happened."

"But that doesn't make sense, Bessica," my mom said.

"She wears a dog collar, Mom. And her boots have tape all over them. She's not a very logical person."

My mom stood up and I watched her deposit a wad of my socks in the hamper. "If this turns into something more, I want you to come to me," she said. "I want you to know that you have a safe place."

I did not know what to say in response to that. I felt like I was trapped inside a soap opera. My mother had never been this dramatic before.

"That's cool," I said.

She walked to my door. "I'm going to pack your lunch tomorrow, okay?"

"Sure," I said. "Will it have cookies in it?"

"It will have grapes," my mother said. "They have a lot of antioxidants."

And as soon as she shut the door, I felt very relieved. But then I realized it was almost time for me to go to bed, and I hadn't talked to Sylvie yet or practiced any cheerleader moves beyond almost-splits, and I felt anxious again. I knew what I needed to do. I needed to take my cell phone and sneak outside and call Sylvie so that when I yelled, my parents didn't hear me. Then I needed to yell at Sylvie and dump out all my anger. And after I was finished doing that, I needed to come back inside my house, do some homework, attempt to kick myself out of a back bend, and sleep.

I cracked open my bedroom door. My parents were watching the news. And it wasn't even the local news. It was one of those stations that broadcasts the news twenty-four hours a day. All the time. Earthquakes. Puppies flushed down toilets. Hostage situations. That station was such a bummer.

I opened the door as quietly as I could and sneaked outside. At first I thought I would call Sylvie from my garage. But then I worried about the echo. So I went into my backyard. But then things felt spooky. It was totally dark and a little windy and I could hear an owl. Plus, it was cold. I walked around my backyard to try to warm up. Then I was hit by a good idea. Sometimes Noll left his Mustang unlocked. I could go sit in there and call Sylvie. I hurried to the car.

When I got to the Mustang it was looking very shiny, even in the pitch-black darkness. I climbed inside and sat there for a minute to make sure that I wasn't going to get caught right away. Apparently, I was in the clear. So I called Sylvie. As her phone rang I became very nervous.

I didn't want her mom to answer. I wanted Sylvie to answer. But the thought of talking to Sylvie made me nervous too, which was weird. Because before her mother put us on a friendship break, I used to talk to Sylvie several times a day.

"Hello?" a voice said.

I couldn't believe it. It was Sylvie. But instead of wanting to yell at her, I wanted to talk to her.

"Sylvie!" I said. "It's me! Bessica!"

"Bessica! How are you? What are you doing?"

"I'm sitting in Noll Beck's car," I said.

"What?"

"It's cool," I said. "I just got spooked by the darkness and the wind and an owl. All that hooting. So I needed to sit inside something."

"Why didn't you call me from your house?" she asked.

And I thought about telling her that I needed to be someplace where I could yell, but I worried that might sound rude. So I changed the topic.

"Sylvie, how are things going at South? What do you think about PE and your dress code?" I wondered if she had to wear green pants. I wondered if her PE class was pukier than mine.

"I'm not taking PE," Sylvie said.

And I got a little bit excited. Because I wanted to hear

her excuse. Maybe I could use it and get out of my class. "Cool! What's your excuse?"

"I don't have one. I'm taking dance. It counts for PE."

This seemed totally unfair. "Dance?" I asked. My school didn't even offer that. "Do you jog in there?"

Sylvie laughed. "No. We dance."

"Like, the cha-cha, or the rumba, or what?" I asked.

Sylvie and I had watched a dance show on TV before. It was thrilling for ten minutes. Then it appeared to be the same thing happening over and over. But Sylvie had really liked it. That's how we ended up in our tap-dance clinic.

"I have to identify and execute axial and locomotor steps," Sylvie said.

"Bummer," I said. Hearing this made me feel a little bit better. Because, while it might not have been as bad as jogging, that sounded like a rotten way to spend fifty-four minutes.

"I love it," Sylvie said. "In a couple of weeks we're going to practice using different kinds of energetic movement, like swing, collapse, suspend, and explode."

That did sound like fun. Especially the suspend and explode part. "I'm jogging all the time."

"I bet you're in great shape!" Sylvie said.

But I didn't really care about my shape. Because then Sylvie started talking about her other classes. And it sounded like she really liked them. I had expected to hear that things were going terrible and that she missed me and was considering going on a hunger strike. But that was not the direction this conversation took.

"I love every single thing about South," she said. "How's North?"

"Wait," I said. "I think we have a bad connection. Because I thought I just heard you say that you loved every single thing about South." That was so rude. Because *I* wasn't at South. Did she love that part too?

"Uh-huh," Sylvie said. "I love *everything*. So what's North like? Who are you hanging out with?"

I could not believe that Sylvie was enjoying middle school. That wasn't fair. She should have been suffering as much as I was. Maybe more.

"I hang out with my friends," I lied. I did not mention loner town.

"You'll never guess who I'm spending a lot of time with," Sylvie said. "Malory Mahoney."

"Malory Mahoney the Big Plastic Phony?" I asked. Because Sylvie and I couldn't stand her. She was superfake and was a huge blabbermouth!

"Yeah," Sylvie said. "She's actually really nice."

"What about the fact that she told on Dee Washington for hiding the chalk that day? Or Maven Hollis for freeing the class gerbil into the wild? She's awful!"

"Don't say that," Sylvie said. "Malory's my friend. We all make mistakes."

"Are you being serious?" I asked. I hoped she was making a really lame joke.

"I thought you said that the cool thing about middle school was being able to start brand new. Shouldn't that be true for Malory too?" Sylvie asked.

When Sylvie asked me this, I started to gag.

"Are you okay?" Sylvie asked.

"Actually," I said, "I'm not. I need to talk to you about something very, very important."

"Okay," Sylvie said. "But get to it, because if my mom finds me talking to you I'll be in big trouble. She's still enforcing the friendship break."

I rolled my eyes. Wasn't I important to Sylvie at all?

"It's about the diary," I said. "I need to know exactly what those ten pages have written on them besides your ocean pictures. And I also need to know the names of everybody you've shown those pages to. And I also need to know the names of everybody who you lent our collaborative diary to before you ripped out those pages and threw our collaborative diary away. Also, I need to know if you let these people make photocopies."

There was a pause. "Besides my mom, nobody has seen the ten pages," Sylvie said. "And I never lent the diary to anybody."

When I heard this, I started to feel myself getting a little mad.

"You need to be honest with me," I said. "My whole reputation is on the line." Because while she might have been dancing around South and being pals with Malory Mahoney, my existence at North was a whole lot tougher.

"I am being honest with you," Sylvie said. "I never let anybody see it. Ever. My mom accidentally found those pages."

Then I started getting very worried that Malory Mahoney the Big Plastic Phony had turned my friend into a big phony too. Because there was no way this could be the truth. I took a deep breath.

"Sylvie, if you tell me the names of all the people right now, I promise I won't yell at you. And I might even forgive you." But I didn't know if that was true. Because I really, really wanted to yell at Sylvie and be mad at her forever.

"I told you," Sylvie said. "I didn't show it to anybody!"

I was breathing so hard that I was fogging up the windows in Noll's Mustang.

"Sylvie," I said. "I don't like calling you a liar."

"Then don't."

"I bumped into a girl today who told me that she'd read the diary from cover to cover. She said that you'd lent it to her. So did you lend her the ten pages or the whole thing?" I never should have let Sylvie keep those stupid ten pages.

"What?" Sylvie asked. "She's lying."

"No," I said. "I think she's seen everything! Because she knows about everything! Our toe prints. Your fart-bubble drawings. Even Kettle Harris!" I was stretching the truth. But it was almost all the way true. And I really wanted to pressure Sylvie into coming clean.

"That's impossible. She's lying!" Sylvie said. "What's this girl's name?"

That was when I realized that I didn't even know her name.

"Let's just call her fluffy-ponytail girl. And let's just say that I trust her."

"Well, you shouldn't! Because I'm telling you the truth! Maybe she went inside the hole and got it."

"Sylvie, that hole has farm equipment parked on it now. And she said that you lent it to her."

I didn't enjoy lying. But it was necessary.

But Sylvie wouldn't budge. "It. Is. Impossible."

And this was when I got very mad. Because I knew it wasn't impossible at all. I knew it was very possible. Because it was true. And Malory Mahoney had turned Sylvie into a plastic phony.

"Why did you show people our diary?" I asked. "That was personal stuff."

"I didn't!"

"You did!" I said.

"You're wrong!"

By this point I was yelling very loudly.

"I am not wrong! Fluffy-ponytail girl read the whole thing! And she mocked me in the principal's office."

"This doesn't make any sense!" Sylvie said in a sad, pleading way. "And why were you in the principal's office?"

That was when I realized that somebody was standing outside the car. And instead of getting frightened that a stranger could be standing there, I became frightened that Noll Beck was standing there. And I was right.

"Holy crud!" I said.

"What?" Sylvie asked.

"Noll Beck is standing right here!"

"Oh no!" Sylvie said. "You're going to look like an idiot. Get out of there."

"Bessica Lefter, is that you?" Noll asked as he tapped on the window.

"He's tapping on the window!" I said. "And he knows it's me."

"That's terrible," Sylvie said. "Uh-oh. My mom is coming!"

Then I heard the phone click and Sylvie was gone, and I wasn't too surprised because Sylvie had abandoned me before. It was her new favorite way to react when I needed her. I opened the door and the cold air whooshed inside the car.

"What are you doing?" Noll asked. "Are you taking my quarters?"

I looked down at his ashtray. It was stuffed with them.

"No," I said. "I'm having a private conversation." I held up my cell phone as evidence.

"I don't think it's a good idea for you to be in my car," Noll said. "If you knocked it into gear, you could roll out into the road."

"I would never knock your car into gear," I said.

A girl stepped out of the darkness. She was standing next to Noll. She was tall. And blond. And gorgeous. "Do you live nearby?" she asked.

I wanted to die. I knew that Noll dated. But I never thought I'd meet his girlfriends this way.

"Yes," I said.

"Did you sneak out here to talk to your boyfriend?" she asked.

"Yes," I lied. Because that made me look so much cooler than my real explanation.

"She is so cute," the girl said. "I love your hair."

I reached up and touched it. "It's a pixie cut."

"You look like a doll!" she said.

And I didn't know how to respond to that. Because I

wasn't a fan of dolls. Especially ones with ceramic heads. When it came to toys, which I rarely played with anymore, I liked kites.

"Bessica," Noll said. "Please stay out of my car."

And the way he said it hurt my feelings. Because it was clear that he had no desire for me to ever be inside his car. I climbed out of it and brushed past him. I wanted to tell him and his girlfriend to have a good night. But I didn't. It was just too awkward.

I sneaked back into my house and curled up on my bed and thought about what Sylvie had said. She sounded so convincing when she told me that she hadn't lent our journal to people. And that was painful. Because I wanted to believe her, but I also knew the truth. The fluffy-ponytail girl knew all about Kettle Harris. And that meant Sylvie was a liar. And what was really terrible wasn't that she was lying to other people. I could have handled that. Because that was something I sometimes did. But Sylvie Potaski was lying to me. And that felt rotten. All night long, I tossed and turned. All night long, I felt so alone.

# CHAPTER 18

I got ready for school the next morning in a very grumpy mood. When it came time for me to pick out a color for my sneaker tongues, I chose black to reflect how terrible I felt about life.

"Are you excited for cheerleading practice?" my mom asked. She'd gotten up a little bit earlier than usual and made me pancakes.

"That's not till Friday," I said. I plopped down in my chair so hard that I accidentally moved it.

My mother flipped a pancake onto my plate and frowned. "I thought you had tumbling practice today."

I took my plate and started drowning my pancake in

maple syrup. "That's true. But tumbling practice is part of PE, because Ms. Penrod believes that fitness is all about adding variety and avoiding heartbreaking grass stains." I looked at my mom and smiled. "I love pancakes."

"I know." She sat down next to me and watched me eat. "Are you nervous about tumbling?"

I shook my head. "Why should I be? We'll be doing it on mats."

"Right. But if Ms. Penrod asks you to do something that you're not comfortable doing, it's okay to tell her that inverting yourself makes you queasy." My mom pointed to her stomach when she said this.

I rolled my eyes. Ever since I got sick on an upside-down roller coaster, my mom thought I had trouble inverting myself. "Ms. Penrod isn't teaching the class. Alice Potgeiser is."

"Who's that?"

I finished my pancake and looked down at my syrup puddle. "A stuck-up person who is really good at tumbling. Can I have another pancake?"

My mother flipped a second pancake onto my plate and set my lunch sack down next to me. It was not emitting any odor, so I couldn't tell what kind of sandwich it was.

"I made you a turkey and cheese sandwich."

"With cookies?" I asked.

"No. With turkey and cheese and mustard." My mom

smiled at me like she'd told a funny joke, but I thought it was lame.

I made a serious face. "Will I ever get cookies? I mean, don't I deserve cookies?"

My mother watched me saw apart the last of my pancake. "Maybe you'll get cookies next time. Today you got grapes."

"Wonderful," I said. But I didn't mean it. "Hey. Do I have a postcard from Grandma that you forgot to give me?"

"No. But I bet you get one soon."

"Are you saying that because you know she sent me one, or are you just guessing?" I asked.

"I'm guessing," she said. "But knowing your grandma, you'll have another one soon."

"I better," I said. Because if a person abandons you during a very difficult time in your life, the least that person can do is write you all the time. "And I don't want to hear about the great time she's having with Willy." I pictured him falling off the tallest mountain ever.

"Ease up on Willy," my mom said.

What a terrible thing to tell me first thing in the morning. I rolled my eyes and put my sticky dish in the stupid sink.

All day long I was pretty thrilled about learning how to tumble so that I could improve my chances at becoming a cheerleader. It was hard to focus on anything. Nutrition was boring. English was a bummer. Math involved a quiz that was horrific. Lunch was lonely. Geography was awful. And it sort of felt like public speaking would never end.

For PE, I think I was the fastest one to change. I didn't have time to mess around and get my socks perfectly level. I put on my gear and rushed to the mats, because I needed to learn as much about tumbling as possible so that I could kick all the other wannabes' butts and take my rightful spot at the cheerleaders' table in the lunchroom.

Once I was on the mats, I started looking around for Alice Potgeiser. I figured she would look like one of the best tumblers in the world. That was when I made a terrible discovery and saw somebody I didn't want to see. I spotted the fluffy-haired girl who'd read my diary and knew that I liked Kettle. She was standing right next to Ms. Penrod—talking to her! Why was she even here?

Then I discovered something worse. Ms. Penrod called the fluffy-haired girl by her name. And it was the worst name imaginable: Alice Potgeiser! I gasped. Could my life get any worse? Yes. Because as soon as I learned the true identity of the expert tumbler, I also learned that she had a minor thumb injury and would not be teaching us how to tumble this week.

"In three weeks we will be introduced to intermediate tumbling," Ms. Penrod said.

But that didn't help me at all. Because I needed to be

introduced to it right away. So I could learn it for cheer-leading tryouts. I was so mad at Alice's stupid minor thumb injury. I bet she hurt it by doing something dumb. Like using her thumb too much. I stared at Alice as she happily hopped off the mats and out the door. Stupid expert tumbler. Then things got a little weird. Instead of doing regular PE stuff, like no-fun jogging around the gym, my nutrition teacher showed up. Except she wasn't dressed in her cowgirl clothes. She was wearing tight, stretchy black clothes. Sort of what I'd expect an acrobat to wear.

"I wonder why she's here," I said.

I guess Ms. Penrod heard me, because she said, "Mrs. Mounds is going to teach us some basic yoga moves."

"That's right," Mrs. Mounds said. She smiled so big her face looked like it could split in two. "Find a comfortable position on the mat. Make sure that you've got enough room to stretch out."

So I walked toward a corner and found myself plenty of room.

"Take off your shoes and socks," Mrs. Mounds said.

This was so not good. Because I wasn't prepared to show people my bare feet. I hadn't cut my toenails in ages. What was wrong with Mrs. Mounds? But everybody around me took off their socks and shoes, and so I did too.

"Now, with your feet shoulder-width apart, reach forward," she said. "Breathe in joy. Exhale gratitude."

When I reached forward, I breathed like a normal person. But Mrs. Mounds didn't. She made very loud whooshing sounds.

"Close your eyes and release a juicy breath," Mrs. Mounds said.

I did not do either of those things. I kept hoping that at some point we would put our socks and shoes back on and learn cheerleader moves. But that didn't happen.

"Reach! Juicy breath! Reach!" she pleaded.

I glanced at Ms. Penrod. Even though she was squatty, she was an excellent reacher and releaser of juicy breaths.

"We will now do a basic yoga move that will help you improve your circulation and overall health. Place your palms on the mat. Spread your fingers and keep your legs straight. Lift your derriere," she said. "Lift! Lift! This is downward-facing dog."

And I did that. But it did not feel normal. It felt like I was poking my butt in the sky, and I never realized that that was something people did to improve their circulation or health. Just then I heard a ton of squeaking shoes. And because all the girls had taken off their shoes, I knew that the people squeaking around the gym were not girls from my class. Even though I was upside down, I turned and looked.

Holy crud! The boys were here! They were never in the gym when we were in the gym. They were supposed to be in the weight room lifting heavy stuff in order to grow muscles. Why did they show up when I was facing downward like a dog with my butt sticking out? Why was Mrs. Mounds doing this to us? Didn't she remember what it felt like to be a sixth grader with a butt? You didn't poke it in the air in front of boys. I dropped to the mat and curled up like a ball.

"Good job, Bessica," Mrs. Mounds said. "Listen to your body. Return to child's pose when you need a break."

Then I felt more eyes on me than had ever been on me in my life. Even though I didn't want to see who was looking at me, I lifted my head. It was terrible. All three psychobullies were standing right there. Laughing. And so was Dolan the Puker. What was he laughing at? And Blake was standing there too, holding a jump rope. Why didn't we jump rope in PE? Why was I doing yoga in front of boys? Then everybody else in my class dropped into balls like me.

"This is a great asana to stretch the hips. But this is not a good asana to practice if you are suffering from a knee injury or diarrhea. Up again. Push back into your dogs."

And when they all pushed back up into downward-facing dog, I didn't want to join them. I wanted to stay where I was. Ball. Ball. Ball. So I did. Until it was time for us to assume something called the corpse pose, where we lay on our backs until class ended. Mrs. Mounds called it *savasana*. It was supposed to do something for our chakras. But I didn't care. Because I didn't see how this would help me become a cheerleader at all.

"Mom! Mom!" I said when I got home. But she was still at work. I opened the refrigerator to see if there were any leftover pancakes. But there weren't. Then I checked the counter for a postcard from Grandma. But there was only a dish towel. So I grabbed my phone and went to my room and called the one person who I thought could save my life from turning into total crud. I called Marci Docker. Because she knew how cheerleaders operated. And I needed to know that immediately.

> **Me:** Marci, I need your advice. This is
> Bessica Lefter and I'm very stressed
> out about cheerleading tryouts. Alice
> Potgeiser was supposed to teach us
> intermediate tumbling today. But I
> learned basic yoga moves instead.
> **Marci:** Bummer. Alice is a tumbling ge-
> nius.
> **Me:** I know it's a bummer, but what
> should I focus on?
> **Marci:** Have you been practicing?
> **Me:** Yes and no.
> **Marci:** Can you do a round-off yet?

**Me:** No.

**Marci:** Can you do a cartwheel?

**Me:** Yes! Yes! I can do, like, four in a row.

**Marci:** That's a start. Do you have good lift?

**Me:** Probably.

**Marci:** Try to jump off the ground and tell me how high you get.

**Me:** (*Oomph. Oomph.*) I can get knee-level.

**Marci:** Can you kick your legs out while you jump in the air?

**Me:** Let me try. (*Oomph! Ugh!*)

**Marci:** Are you all right?

**Me:** I can't kick my legs out while I jump. I can only jump.

**Marci:** That's too bad.

**Me:** Don't say that. I believe in positive visualization. It's something my grandma taught me. If I picture myself doing something over and over, I'm usually always able to do it. Eventually.

**Marci:** That's cool. Then you should visualize yourself doing the splits, and round-offs, and kicking your legs out straight when you jump. Hey. I'm on a date, so I better go.

**Me:** Oh my heck! I didn't know you were on a date.

**Marci:** We're eating tacos. Dial me later. Tootles. (*Click.*)

**Me:** Sure thing!

After I hung up with Marci, I pictured myself doing all sorts of cheerleader moves. And I was pretty good. It was like there was a movie going on inside my head and it was starring me. As a cheerleader. When my mom got home I was still practicing the power of positive visualization. She opened my door and looked at me.

"Are you napping?" she asked.

"No," I said. "My eyes are open."

"Did you have a good day?"

I bolted upright and pointed at her. "I did not. In PE we learned basic yoga moves, and all the boys came out to watch us and I had my butt in the air and got laughed at because that's how you do downward-facing dog!"

My mother blinked at me. "Yoga? They're teaching you yoga in middle school? You're lucky. When I took PE it was all about push-ups and the flexed-arm hang."

Then my mom left and it became clear to me that she

was not the ally she used to be. I followed her into the hallway to complain a little more.

"Did you miss the part where I told you that my butt was poking straight up in the air?"

"Oh, Bessica, I'm sorry. But I had a tough day at work. Shirley has the flu, so I'm handling everything."

Shirley worked in the podiatrist's office with my mom. She was part-time and sometimes forgot the order of the alphabet and filed things wrong. I wanted to complain more about *my* day, but I couldn't because my mom wanted to complain more about *her* day.

"And there are some complications with Betty."

"Mallet-toe Betty?" I asked.

"She got an infection."

"That's disgusting."

My mother slipped off her jacket and slumped down on the couch. "It happens."

"Can I get you something? Like a carrot?" I'd seen a bunch of those in the refrigerator while I was looking for leftover pancakes.

My mom shook her head. "Maybe you could gather the mail."

"Yeah," I said. I was actually surprised that I hadn't done that already. I dashed outside, pulled open the mailbox, and grabbed a big wad of what looked like bills. There was also a postcard from Grandma. Even though it was cold outside, I stood on the lawn and read it. There was a picture of an enormous spoon scooping up a cherry. It looked like a sculpture. Then the back of the card told me it was a sculpture from the Minneapolis Sculpture Garden, and I felt pretty brilliant for already guessing that.

Bessica!

Here is a cherry that weighs twelve hundred pounds. Doesn't it look good? Your grandma said you liked cherries so I thought you might like this card. I hope you do! Life is short and cherries are great.

See you soon and hope you're well,

Willy

Bessica Lefter
1556 Beesley Road
Sugar City, Idaho
83448

Huh? Why was Willy sending me a card? I didn't want a card from him. What a jerk! I pictured him falling off a cliff very quickly four times. Then I looked at the picture on the front of the postcard again. It was the worst postcard ever. I stuck it in with the bill wad and went back inside the house.

"Grandma is traveling around with a crazy person," I said. "He just sent me a postcard of a giant cherry that said stupid things."

I turned the corner and saw that my mom had fallen asleep. Her head was tilted to one side and her mouth was open a little bit. I quietly set the mail down on the coffee table and sneaked into the hallway. Then I stood there because I didn't know what to do with myself. I kept thinking about stupid Willy and Grandma. It was like she'd gone off with Willy and become a whole new person. And that wasn't so hot for me, because I liked her the way she was before she left.

I stomped downstairs as quietly as I could. Even though I wanted to find Grandma a new boyfriend, it was clear to me that it was a waste of my time. I needed to just give up and accept the fact that sometimes the people you love most, like best friends and grandmas, can zoom out of your life and go insane in the blink of an eye.

I opened up Grandma's account so I could delete everything and turn her status back to inactive. She now had over one hundred emails. It hurt so much when I deleted them all and dumped them in the account's trash can. I didn't want to send her future boyfriends there. But that was where they went. Stupid potential boyfriends. When I was finished dumping everybody in the trash, I climbed the stairs to my room.

I still had a lot of homework. Also, I'd visualized myself

doing the splits a ton, but I hadn't practiced doing them on the floor in a very long time. So I did that. And I got much closer to the carpet than I ever had before. I bounced a little and I almost touched. I felt so relieved. I wasn't going to have to live in loner town after all. I didn't need Alice Potgeiser to teach me basic and intermediate tumbling. I was plenty bendy without her. And I had a feeling that once I became a cheerleader, once I had an automatic lunch table full of friends, all the terrible stuff in middle school would finally turn good.

## THINGS TO DO TO PREVENT MY LIFE FROM TURNING TO TOTAL CRUD

1. Write off Sylvie
2. Become a cheerleader
3. Force Raya Papas to become my friend
4. Learn more

# CHAPTER 19

**E**ven though it was dark and cold oustide the morning of cheerleading practice, I did not feel doomed. I climbed out of bed and hurried into the kitchen to grab a handful of cereal to wake me up. And when I did this I saw something on the counter that made me very happy. It was a package from Grandma! On the outside she'd written in big blue inky letters,

PLEASE GIVE THIS TO BESSICA
THE FIRST DAY OF
CHEERLEADING PRACTICE.

When I read that, I knew it was okay for me to tear it open. So I did, as fast as I could.

Grandma was a genius. Inside that package was a pair of purple stretch pants that I could wear for PE. This was a big relief. Because I still hadn't figured out where to buy purple pants. I felt the material between my fingers to make sure that it wasn't the kind that would itch. And it wasn't. Holding my purple PE stretch pants made me miss Grandma in a very powerful way. It would have been so nice to have her here with me. That was when I realized that deleting those emails was the worst mistake I had ever made in my life. Because getting rid of Willy had been the right idea.

I ran downstairs, opened her account, and went straight to her trash. How could I have made such a terrible mistake? I hoped with my whole heart that her future boyfriends were still inside her trash can. *Click. Click. Click.* And they were! I carefully moved them back into her inbox, where they belonged.

Even though I shouldn't have, I read the emails. It was pretty obvious that the responders liked sandwiches and Grandma. One possibility named Sully was a retired engineer who wanted to see Grandma next week when he was in Rexburg. That was a huge bummer. Because Sully couldn't see Grandma next week while he was in Rexburg, because Grandma was riding around the middle of America in a stupid Winnebago. Poor Sully.

I decided to set something up for when Grandma would be back, in four weeks. I worried about how to phrase it, though, because I didn't want to sound like me. I wanted to sound like Grandma. Also, I wasn't sure how many men Grandma should agree to meet. Because I still wanted her to have plenty of time to spend with me. I tapped my fingers on the desk and tried to think strategically.

Four seemed like a good number. It was easy to find the best four. Engineer Sully. And Pete who lived in Post Falls and wanted to take Grandma on a hike in the Kaniksu National Forest. Because forests were cool. And Hunter who lived in The Dalles, Oregon, and who wanted to take Grandma on a visit to Mount Hood. Because visits only lasted a couple of days and then Grandma would be back home. And Pilot Mike who lived in Missoula, Montana. He was my favorite, because he had an awesome personality.

In his subject line he said that he wanted to take Grandma waterskiing. I clicked on his picture. Holy crud! It was too good to be true. In addition to being a former pilot, and sending a gorgeous picture of himself, he had also included a fantastic picture of his superhuge boat. In fact, I think it was a yacht. And he'd named it the SS *Funshine*.

His message was wonderful.

Glad to hear you like boats and
adventure, Rhoda. Getting together for a sandwich sounds
great. Give me your phone number and we can set it up. You're
not like a lot of the other people
I've met on this site. You've got
the heart of a kid and the legs of
a supermodel.

I read Pilot Mike's message seven more times. Plus, I couldn't stop looking at his boat. It was like he really understood who Grandma was. When I closed my eyes, I could picture us all together aboard the SS *Funshine*. Grandma and I were so happy. And so was this Mike person. That was when I decided to write Pilot Mike a letter that was straight from the heart. Grandma's heart.

Dear Mike, Thanks for the delightful email. I'm shy about giving out my phone number. Why
don't you send me yours. Sandwiches sound wonderful. Maybe
we can eat them on board the SS
Funshine.
Tootles. Rhoda.

When I sent that message I didn't feel bad at all. I felt like I'd figured out a great solution for returning Grandma to normal. Because Grandma hadn't made Grandma go crazy. Willy had done that. And so if I introduced her to Pilot Mike, who seemed very normal, Grandma would most likely return to her own self again.

When I finally ran upstairs, I was very behind.

"Bessica, you're not even dressed," my mom said. "Are you sick?"

I dashed to my room. "No, I feel great." I threw on my clothes as fast as I could. Then I attached my blue tongues to my sneakers and ran to the kitchen table. I was breathing hard.

"I made you lunch again," my mother said.

"Cool." I wolfed down two pieces of toast.

"It's a hummus sandwich." My mother sat down next to me with a brown paper sack.

"What's it made out of?" I asked.

"Chickpeas!" She smiled and made an *mmm* sound.

I looked out the window into the dark morning. It felt like the middle of the night. My mother's hair was stuck to her head and she had bags under her eyes.

"Maybe you should go back to bed," I said. "I won't miss the bus. I'm hurrying."

She shook her head and poured us each a glass of orange juice. "We have a few minutes before your bus. Let's chat."

I took my glass. "Chat?"

"You haven't talked about any of your friends at school."

"Sylvie goes to South and we're still on the outs. Big-time," I said.

"We're two weeks into school. I'm talking about your friends at North."

I did not want to admit to my mom that I hadn't made any real friends yet. And that currently I was a socially certified nothing.

"Who do you hang out with?" She smiled at me in a very hopeful way.

My mom had bad timing. If she asked me this question in a week, I could tell her about all my cheerleader friends. But I didn't even know their names yet. "Raya Papas."

"That's a pretty name. Tell me about her."

"She likes stickers and she's very alert in math."

"Oh!" my mother said. "She's got a brain for numbers."

"Yeah," I said. "I also spend time with Cameron Bon Qui Qui."

"She sounds interesting."

"I think she wants to grow up to be a policewoman. She likes rules."

"Kids are so mature these days."

I nodded. Then I changed the subject, because I got tired

of lying about the friends I didn't really have. "How's mallet-toe Betty?"

"She needs another casserole. We should probably stop by there today or tomorrow."

Normally, I would have objected to this idea. But I was tired. And maybe when my mom went there, I could hang out with Betty's coward dog and spy on Raya some more and figure out why she was rude to me.

"I forgot to tell you something," my mom said. "Noll came over last night."

And when my mom said this, my heartbeat zoomed. "Noll came to see me?" I asked in a very surprised voice. Because I was pretty sure that after the Mustang incident Noll thought I was a huge dork who might not have been totally normal.

"No. He brought you something." My mother lifted up a card.

My mouth dropped open. "Noll Beck brought me a card last night?"

It seemed impossible, but maybe this was his way of telling me that he'd broken up with his girlfriend and was interested in spending time with me.

"No," my mother said. "The mailman delivered a post-card from Grandma to Noll's house by mistake."

My heart stopped zooming and I took the card. It had a big cow on it.

"What's with the cow?" I asked.

"I think it's a tourist attraction. Apparently, it's the world's largest Holstein."

The cow was named Sue. And she was black and white and had horns and a big udder. The card said she was made out of fiberglass and stood thirty-eight feet tall.

As Mom loaded my lunch into a brown paper sack, she finally noticed that I'd opened my present.

"Bessica! You opened it."

I set the card down and nodded. "It was mine."

"What did Grandma give you?"

"PE pants." They were folded up in the chair next to me, so I lifted them up and showed her.

"You're going to wear those to PE?" my mom asked. Her face looked concerned.

"Totally," I said. "My teacher said I have to wear purple pants. It's in our dress code. It's part of our grade."

But my mom's face only looked more worried. "Have you read what's written on the backside?"

It hadn't occurred to me that something could be written on the backside. I turned them over and read the butt. KISS THIS. I gasped.

"I think that might actually violate a decency rule," my mom said.

I didn't know if it violated one of those, but I sure wasn't going to wear purple pants that said KISS THIS during PE in the school gymnasium. What was Grandma thinking? "What are they even good for?" I asked. I tossed them back on the chair.

"Pajamas. Or long underwear," my mom offered.

"Long underwear?" That seemed like a terrible idea. I liked my underwear regular length.

"They're thin enough that if you needed an extra layer for warmth you could wear these underneath your pants."

I could not imagine ever needing an extra layer. "That's weird."

I left the pants and got up and loaded all my stuff into my backpack for school, even Grandma's postcard. And I felt really anxious, because I hadn't slept enough and my purple pants were lame and while I was thrilled about Pilot Mike, I wished I were able to be more honest with my mom about stuff. I started shoving everything into my backpack in a rough manner that resembled mashing.

"You should pack up before you go to bed," my mom suggested.

I shoved my last book inside my backpack and tugged the zipper closed. "Sure I should."

"Have a good day!" my mom called.

As I walked out to the bus, it was sort of like I couldn't control my own legs. Because I saw Noll's car, and even though I knew I should stay pretty far away from it, I couldn't help myself. I wanted to see if his girlfriend had left anything in there. Because if she had, I thought it would mean they were pretty serious, because she knew she'd be returning to the car. But if she hadn't, then I thought it would mean that they weren't very serious at all.

I hurried up to the passenger-side window and looked inside. The chemistry book was back. And there were more crumpled-up papers in the backseat. And there was a duffel bag in the backseat. I leaned in closer. But I couldn't see what was inside of it because it was zipped shut. Maybe it was the girlfriend's duffel bag. This made me feel terrible. But the duffel bag was red. Would a girl want a red duffel bag? I hoped not.

As I walked away from Noll's car to catch the bus, I knew that it was going to be hard for me to concentrate at school. Because I had a lot on my plate.

All day I was in a distracted mood. I had a tough time remembering my locker combination. And I forgot to automatically give Redge a pen and he had to remind me.

"Hey. Pen girl. I'm waiting."

And when Mrs. Mounds lectured about the central nervous system, I only took half as many notes as I should have. And when Mr. Val had us read a story out loud in class about a celebrated jumping frog, I couldn't follow what was happening, even though he turned off the flute music. When the bell rang and class ended, I was surprised to see people leaving the room, because it felt like we'd just gotten there. And I was so distracted in math that I accidentally sat in Raya Papas's seat.

"You're in my seat," she said.

"Really?" I asked. And then I didn't move right away because I sort of wanted Raya to talk to me more.

"You need to move," Raya said.

"Okay." But I stayed right there.

"Do I need to get the teacher?"

I shook my head and got up.

"You might not look alt, but you sure act alt," Raya said. "You're totally weird."

And I didn't understand why Raya was being so mean to me, because I was nice to her. And I liked her. So I thought she should have been automatically kind to me until we became friends and she wrote me notes with heart stickers on them.

After that, the only interesting thing that happened in math was that Raya told the story of her neighbor's dog getting snatched by a dangerous coyote.

"He got grabbed right by the mailbox!" Raya said. And she didn't tell just one person. She told everybody. And so that became a very, very popular topic in class.

*Coyote. Coyote. Coyote. Dog. Dog. Dog.* It's all anybody wanted to talk about.

I'd seen a coyote once with my dad. It had big teeth and

looked exactly like a wild animal. I wasn't surprised that it would snatch a dog. When the bell rang, I went straight to my locker. And when I opened my locker, I took out my lunch sack, and I was bummed out. Because my hummus sandwich was releasing an odor.

I reached inside my backpack and was really surprised by what came tumbling out of it. First, Grandma's postcard fell to the floor. It was very bent. Then my cell phone dropped down there too. Uh-oh. I remembered the postcard, but I'd hurried so fast to pack for school that I must've accidentally stuffed my phone in my backpack. I picked it up and stuck it in my lunch sack along with the postcard. Because I sort of felt like calling somebody. Because lunch was a lonely time for me. I slammed my locker shut and I saw somebody inside Davis's locker. I figured it was Davis. He gave me a strange look.

"What's in that bag?" Davis asked. "Is it a dead animal?"

I didn't mention my banned cell phone. "I'm Bessica. This is my lunch. It's made out of chickpeas."

"That's disgusting," he said. "I'd rather eat my own arm."

And I was glad that Davis said that. Because it showed that he was most definitely a dork. And so I walked off and didn't say another word to him. I headed toward the row. And on my way there a terrible thing happened. I ran into Cola.

"Are you going to walk? Or are you going to run? Or are you going to attack the vending machine?" he asked.

That psycho-bully was such a goon. I didn't even know what to say to him. So I just said a fact. "I brought my lunch today."

Then Redge and Beecher appeared.

"What's that smell?" Beecher asked.

And I didn't mention that it was my sandwich.

"What's in your bag?" Cola asked.

"Lunch," I said.

Then I started walking away, because I didn't want to waste valuable minutes of my life talking to those three.

"I know what's in your bag," Cola said. "A fart sandwich."

Then Cola made loud fart noises over and over. And I just kept walking. But he followed me. And so did Redge and Beecher. And they made fart noises too. So I didn't walk to the row. I walked to the bathroom as fast as I could. Because my eyes felt hot. Like I could cry at any moment. And I didn't want to cry in the hallway. I really didn't want to cry in the bathroom either. But I thought that was my safest option. So I opened a stall and sat down on a toilet. And I watched the tears tumble to the floor in juicy splatters.

I wanted to throw my sandwich away. But I was also hungry. I didn't understand why school had to be this difficult. Or why the psycho-bullies couldn't stop being psycho. Or why rude Raya couldn't start being nice. Or why my mom couldn't have made me a peanut butter sandwich.

I reached over and grabbed some toilet paper and blew my nose. Then I continued to sit there. And I decided to open my smelly bag and eat my smelly sandwich. And that was when a bunch of girls came into the bathroom. Something about what was happening reminded me of my weird dream. I held my breath and peeked through the crack in the door. There were three of them. And one of them was the fluffy-ponytail girl who knew that I liked Kettle. I almost lost my appetite.

"We'll make them do round-offs right away," said a girl wearing green shoes.

"Backflips," said Alice Potgeiser.

"Shouldn't we let them stretch first?" asked a girl wearing red sandals. "Won't they break their necks if we don't?"

"Maybe," Alice said. And then they all laughed. "But we only want the best. No losers who can barely jump."

Then they all laughed some more and left. And I knew they were talking about cheerleading. And I knew that I didn't know how to do round-offs or backflips, even if I did stretch. So it seemed pretty likely that after school today I would break my neck.

I blew my nose again. And then I remembered Grandma's postcard. I reached into my lunch sack and pulled it out. On the back of the cow postcard, Grandma had only written two words: *LIVE LARGE!* I put the postcard back in my bag. What was that supposed to mean? Just because she was off having a fun time with Willy didn't mean that she should send me messages I couldn't understand. *Live large.* What did she want me to do—try out for cheerleading and break my neck? *Live large.* I said it over and over as I sat on the toilet. What a mean thing to send me. Grandma didn't have any clue about how bad things really were. That was when I realized the only solution to this problem. I needed to get my banned phone and call her.

Sadly, I just got her voice mail. She was probably with maniac Willy inside a stupid cave where she didn't get cell phone reception. In addition to hating Willy, I was really starting to hate caves. I left Grandma a message:

"This is Bessica and I'm calling you
from the bathroom because I have
no idea what your cow card means.
Can you please call me as soon as
possible and explain? Also, would
you please consider coming home?

Just *consider* it. Your room is very
empty. Sometimes I go down there
and sit and miss you and feel rotten. In ten minutes I plan to—"

And then I just hung up, because I sort of wanted to
leave Grandma a cliff-hanger message. Because I thought
that might encourage her to call me back sooner. I peeked
out the door at the clock on the wall. Lunch was over in
five minutes. Time flies when you're bummed out on a toilet. I looked at my phone. I felt like calling somebody else.
Then it hit me. I should call Marci Docker and ask her for
more tips about trying out for cheerleading. Because she
was an expert. Also, she was one of the only people whose
number was programmed into my phone. I was so relieved
when she answered!

"This is Bessica Lefter again," I said. I could hear a ton
of noise in the background. I guessed high school was a
loud place. "I just heard some cheerleaders talking about
tryouts and it made me very nervous, and that day we had
lunch you said a lot of helpful things and I was hoping
you could give me some pointers."

There was a little bit of silence. And I was afraid she'd
forgotten who I was. And I was getting ready to talk about
her feet issues and how she knew my mom, but then she
started talking.

"Bessica Lefter, you are too adorable."

"Thank you," I said. I liked the compliment, but what I really needed was guidance. "How important is stretching and what muscles should I stretch first? I'm worried about my neck."

"Don't worry too much about stretching or your neck," she said.

This shocked me, but I figured that Marci knew what she was talking about.

"There are three things you need to do," she said.

I wished I'd brought a pen with me. But I just had half my sandwich, a paper bag, some carrot sticks, and Grandma's postcard. "Tell me slowly."

"Okay. First, show up."

"Right," I said. But that sounded like a no-brainer. I was hoping for the inside scoop.

"Second, be proud and be loud."

"Uh-huh," I said. That made sense. I wanted them to understand that I could cheer at high decibels.

"Third, shake your butt like a wild animal."

"What?" I asked. Because I thought maybe that was code for something.

"A lot of people are afraid to surrender to the costume. You can't be afraid. You have to go out there and act like a wild animal. You've got to grab their laughter. That was my strategy for being the bee."

Then I realized that I was talking to the wrong twin. I was talking to Vicki. The mascot. And so I hadn't gotten any helpful information at all.

"Thanks," I said. "But can I ask one more question?"

"You betcha!"

But then the bell rang, and I was so startled that I snapped my phone shut. Uh-oh. And then I didn't have time to call Vicki again. And I didn't have time to call Marci either. Because lunch was over and I had to get to geography. Because we were going to have a test on the Arctic tundra and its relatively low biodiversity.

# CHAPTER 20

After school ended, I stayed in my PE clothes and got my backpack out of my locker and walked to the gym. It looked like there were about thirty other girls trying out. Last year's cheerleaders didn't have to try out again. That meant there were five spots open, but three of them weren't even real spots. They were alternates. Which meant that you had to learn all the cheers, but you didn't necessarily get to do them in front of people. But you could still eat lunch at the cheerleader table. And that was all I really wanted anyway. There was a poster that said *Sign In Here*. So I walked over and put my name down.

After I did that, I didn't sit with the big clump of girls

trying out. I sat off to the side. I glanced over at the group of kids who were trying out for mascot. There were only a few. Oh my heck! Dolan the Puker was there. I couldn't believe that he wanted to be a bear or a wolf. The last thing any middle school wanted was a puking mascot. Didn't he know that? What was he doing?

"Practice will start in ten minutes!" Alice Potgeiser yelled. She looked so happy and fluffy-haired. I touched my pixie. I didn't regret whacking off all my hair, but sometimes I wished it felt fluffier. Then I unzipped my backpack and reached inside and took out my banned phone. I held it close to me. Sitting off to the side in the gym was tough. Since school was over, I thought it was okay to try Grandma again. So I did.

"Bessica!" Grandma answered.

"How come you didn't call me back?" I asked. I was really surprised I didn't have a message from her already.

"I just got out of a cave."

"Right," I said. I didn't bother asking her about it, because I didn't really care.

"Did you get the pants?" she asked.

"Yeah," I said. "But there's a problem."

"Are they the wrong size?"

"No," I said. "They fit. The problem is the message that's printed on the butt. Mom says it's not decent and I can't wear them in public."

"They're pajamas!" Grandma said. "I didn't think you'd wear them in public. Who wears purple stretch pants in public?"

"My entire PE class," I said. "It's our uniform."

Grandma didn't say anything back, so I kept complaining. I walked farther away from the cheerleaders and toward the mascots, because I didn't want the cheerleaders to hear me being totally negative.

"My life sucks and things are terrible," I said.

"Where are you?"

"The school gymnasium," I said. Then I looked at some of the kids trying out for mascot, shaking their butts, and it made me laugh.

"Are you laughing?" Grandma asked. "Things can't be that terrible."

"Oh, they are," I said. And I didn't explain that I was watching something funny. "It's like everybody in my life is a bull chasing me through a field."

"What are you talking about?"

I couldn't believe that Grandma couldn't remember about the bull. I cleared my throat. "Remember how you told me that Sylvie's mom was like a bull chasing me through a field and I needed to avoid the bull?"

"I do remember that," Grandma said.

Then I heard a crashing sound on the other end of the phone.

"What was that?" I asked. "Where are you?"

"I'm in the motor home. I'm trying to bake Willy a cake for his birthday."

Then I felt worse about everything, because my life was pretty stinky at the moment and I wanted *my grandma* to be at *my house,* baking a cake for *me.*

"If you were here, my life wouldn't be this terrible," I said.

"Bessica, I'll be home in three weeks."

It felt like my own grandma had punched me in the face.

"I'll have been run over by twenty bulls by the time you get here!"

Then it sort of got hard for me to hear, because the mascots were making a ton of noise. They were laughing and pretending to be wolves and bears, and it was out of control and annoying. So I pressed my ear very close to the phone so that I could hear what Grandma was going to say. Because I knew that it would be very kind and loving and inspirational.

"Stop acting like a victim," Grandma said.

I pressed my ear closer to the phone. "I think we have a bad connection. What did you say?"

"Bessica, you're giving away your power."

"Huh?" It was like Grandma had gotten so old that she'd forgotten that sixth graders don't have any power. The eighth graders have the power.

"Mrs. Potaski is a control freak," Grandma said.

And this made me stop breathing a little, because Grandma had never called anybody a freak before.

"Wow," I said. But Grandma kept going.

"You stir her pot, Bessica. Sure, you've made some mistakes. But you're good at heart."

I moved away from the noisy mascots so I wouldn't miss a word of what Grandma was saying. "I am," I said. I watched as the cheerleading hopefuls and current cheerleaders stretched on big green mats on the gymnasium floor.

"You should enjoy middle school," Grandma said.

And I tried to interrupt her and tell her about the psycho-bullies and Cameron Bon Qui Qui and fluffy-haired Alice Potgeiser and rude Raya Papas and alt Nadia, but Grandma didn't let me.

"Look for happiness and you'll find it."

"I don't know if I believe that," I said. Because if Grandma came to math with me, I didn't think that she'd believe it either.

"Bessica, do you know what I hear in the background while we're talking?"

I looked at the stretching girls.

"Cheerleading tryouts?" I asked.

"Laughter," she said.

Then I glanced back at the noisy mascots.

"Sorry," I said. "It's the stupid mascot people."

"Bessica!" Grandma boomed. "Laughter is good. While you're standing there stressed out of your head, there are people who are finding happiness. You should join them."

I glanced at the aspiring mascots. Some of them were crawling on the floor.

"I don't know for sure, because I didn't go to elementary school with them, but I'm pretty sure the people you are referring to are dweebs."

Grandma sighed. "Maybe dweebs are happy people."

I almost gagged. Did Grandma want me to become a dweeb? If I did that, Sylvie would never want to be my friend again. And Noll Beck would lose all interest in me. And I couldn't imagine that I'd truly be happy. Because a part of me would always be bummed out that I was a dweeb.

"I want everybody to like me," I said. "I want to be a cheerleader."

Grandma didn't say anything right away.

"Bessica, I don't think I can support you in your cheer quest."

"What?" I asked.

Grandma had never taken away her support before.

"You don't even like to invert yourself," she said.

She was right. Then I saw a girl try to do a backflip smack her head on the floor, and I gasped.

I realized right then and there that cheerleading was not in my future.

"But I have an hour before Mom picks me up," I said. "Should I just walk around?" I pictured myself walking through the hallways, but that seemed sort of boring. And lonely.

"Do something that will make you happy," Grandma said. Then I heard the sound of an oven door slamming shut.

"Were you making Willy's cake the whole time I was talking to you?" I asked. Because I wanted to think that Grandma would be focused on me the entire time.

"Bessica, I have to go, but will you do me a favor?"

It bugged me that I was having such a miserable day and Grandma was still going to ask me to do something for her.

"What?"

"Lighten up."

"Whatever," I said.

And then Grandma said that she loved me and I said that I loved her and we hung up. Then I walked out into the hallway to get a drink of water and take a break from my life. When I turned the corner, I was very surprised by who I saw.

"Nadia!" I said. "I thought you were suspended."

She shrugged. She was dressed in black clothes and was wearing tinfoil bracelets and had tinfoil around her neck.

She looked more alt than ever. "I have permission to be on the premises. I'm here to pick up homework."

"Cool!" I said. Then I rushed up to her like we were friends. Even though we weren't.

"I was just in the gym, because I was going to try out for cheerleader, but now I think I might not. Because I'm not sure that I want to invert myself. But I also don't want to live in loner town."

Nadia folded her arms across her chest. "Cheerleaders are lame. And loner town has a lot to offer a person. Like your own personal dimly lit space."

"Maybe," I said. I thought of the cheerleaders I'd seen in the bathroom. They had been pretty rude. I thought of the dark hallway that led to the shop classes. Why did anybody want to be socially certified as a nothing? I didn't get it.

"Do you want my advice?" Nadia asked.

And I wasn't sure if I wanted Nadia's advice, but I decided to listen anyway.

"Quit trying to fit in with these farmers. Get a Mohawk. Stand up and stand out."

Then Nadia gave me a peace sign and walked off. And I didn't really think she'd said anything all that useful. Because my pixie was already so short that I didn't think it would make a decent Mohawk.

I walked back into the gym. I didn't want to wander

around the halls. Because that wasn't really making a decision about anything. That was just killing time until my mom showed up. To my right were aspiring cheerleaders. To my left were aspiring mascots. Everybody in both groups seemed very, very eager. I looked back and forth between the two. I felt stuck. But then I saw something that got me unstuck. An aspiring mascot attempted a backbend and fell on her butt, like a total dweeb, and then broke into hysterical laughter, which was apparently how total dweebs reacted to things. I knew which group I needed to pick. I walked over to the cheerleader crowd. And I didn't stay off to the side like I had before. I walked right through everybody. And when I got to the sign-up sheet, I took the pen and scratched off my name. *Hard!* I didn't know if anybody was listening, but I said, "I've decided that I want to be the mascot."

Nobody said anything. But that was okay. I went over to the mascot group and found a place to sit that was nowhere near Dolan the Puker. I sat by a girl with red hair who I had never seen before.

"Hi!" the girl said when I sat down. "I am so nervous. Are you? I'm Maddie. Maddie Bell."

And I nodded, but I didn't say anything. Because I wasn't used to having people talk to me in middle school. Or be nice.

"What's your name?" Maddie asked.

"Bessica Lefter," I said.

Her eyes grew very big. "The girl who kicked in the vending machine?"

I shook my head. "That was Nadia Strom."

But Maddie Bell's eyes stayed big and she moved a little bit away from me. I tried not to take it personally. Then a teacher showed up who was wearing a lot of spandex. "I'm Ms. Rich, the mascot advisor. I'll be teaching you a series of cheers. Word of warning—the mascot position is usually won or lost based on school spirit."

She handed out a piece of paper with a bunch of cheers written on it.

"I have one piece of advice," Ms. Rich said. "When it's your time to shine, you better bring it. Also, make sure you read our cheer sheet. It contains important information."

Reading through the cheer sheet, I noticed there weren't any wolf ones. Dolan noticed this too.

"These are all bear cheers," he said.

Ms. Rich nodded. "We've taken the wolf off the table. There's been a recent spate of coyote attacks. We want to steer clear of animals that resemble wild canines. We want our mascot to be a reassuring symbol of school unity."

And so now that I couldn't be a wolf, I thought about what it would feel like to be a bear. I had to be honest. It felt weird. Then Ms. Rich had us stand up, and she led us in a bunch of fun exercises that involved kicking and leaping and crawling on the floor. And I only looked at the cheerleaders a couple of times. Mostly when I heard a thud or a scream. Luckily, none of them broke their necks. Before I knew it, it was time to go. Ms. Rich explained that we had one final practice before school auditions. She also repeated that we needed to read the cheer sheet. I grabbed my backpack, and when I went outside, my mom was in her car waiting for me. I ran straight to it.

"How was cheer practice?" she asked.

"Forget cheer practice," I said. "I'm trying out for mascot!"

"You're going to be a wolf?" my mom asked.

I shook my head. "Wolves resemble coyotes and they eat local dogs. I'm trying out for the bear."

My mother frowned. "Speaking of local dogs, Betty lost her dog last night to a coyote. He got snatched right by the mailbox."

"I heard about this in math! That's horrible!" I said. "I didn't know it was mallet-toe Betty's coward dog."

My mother sighed. "Can we quit with the labels?"

"Okay," I said. Because I wasn't trying to be mean. Just accurate. "Are you going to bake her another casserole?"

I was afraid that I already knew the answer.

"We'll visit her tomorrow," my mom said.

And then I thought of a great idea. "But I need to practice for mascot!"

"All day?" my mother asked.

"Absolutely," I said.

"You'll miss seeing your friend Raya."

I looked out the window at the hay fields turning yellow. "I can live with that."

# CHAPTER

## 21

When I was practicing for mascot in my bedroom, I realized that Ms. Penrod was right about something. Having the right clothes really did matter. Because I wasn't able to act "bear" enough without looking a little bit like a bear.

I realized this when I put on my dad's winter gloves and it helped me tap into my inner animal. But I needed something more. I explained this to my mom while she made mallet-toe Betty's casserole.

"Having the right athletic gear is essential for optimum performance. That's why I need a furry head," I said, pointing to my pixie.

"You want me to make you a bear costume?" my mom asked.

"Or you can buy me one."

"Do you know how much something like that probably costs?"

"No." I had never seen one at the mall.

My mother poured a can of cream of mushroom soup over a mushy substance. "That looks very gray," I said.

"Well, it tastes delicious."

"When you get back from mallet-toe Betty's, can we go to the craft store and buy fake fur so that we can make me some bear clothes?"

My mother looked down at me with a very frustrated expression. "I only sew hems. I don't know how to make bear clothes."

My mom was really bumming me out. Because we had a sewing machine I was sure we could figure it out. Didn't she want me to win?

"I have a question for you," my mother said. "Have you thought about calling Sylvie?"

I couldn't believe my mom wanted to rub that terrible situation in my face right now. Then I remembered that my mom really didn't know about the entire terrible Sylvie situation.

"I've already called her," I said.

My mother's face broke into a smile as she opened the oven and inserted her gray casserole. "How did it go?"

"Meh." I shrugged and started to leave the room.

"Care to elaborate?"

But I didn't care to do that. So I just kept walking.

"I need to practice. I'm not used to behaving like a wild animal. It's harder than it sounds." Then my mom said something pretty wonderful.

"We can stop by the craft store when I get back from Betty's. Maybe we can make you some fierce paws."

I flipped around and gave my mom a thumbs-up sign. "That sounds awesome! And tell mallet-toe Betty that I say hello. And that middle school hasn't turned me into a potato yet. And tell her to get well soon. And to maybe buy a couch."

"I'll censor that a little," my mom said.

I went to my room and practiced and almost died waiting for Mom to get home from Betty's. At least ten times, I used a pencil to sketch what I felt would be the ideal costume. I needed a furry head. And a furry body. And my legs and arms needed to be extra furry. And in addition to massive amounts of fur, I wanted both my front and back paws to have claws. I was going to look amazing. While all the other wannabe mascots were trying out for mascot looking like normal people, I was going to be trying out for mascot looking like an actual bear.

To help kill time, I did practice some mascot moves. I crawled like a bear. And jumped off furniture like a bear. And I made a ton of bear noises. Also, I looked up bears on the Internet so I could figure out which shade of brown fur to buy. I decided on medium brown, which was a color that would also match my brown sneaker tongues.

I was very relieved when Mom finally came home. So she wouldn't change her mind, I ran right out to the driveway and didn't give her a chance to come in the house. Also, I brought her some crackers.

"Thanks, Bessica," she said, stuffing them in her mouth.

"No, thank *you*!" I said. "I am going to be a bear." When I said this, I sort of sang it a little.

When we arrived at the craft store, I had a hard time waiting until my mom had parked and turned off the car.

"Uh-oh," my mom said.

"What?" I asked. I worried she'd forgotten her purse.

"That's Mrs. Potaski's car."

I followed the aim of my mother's finger. She was right. Mrs. Potaski's big green monster of a car was parked in front of the craft store.

"Is this okay?" she asked.

"It has to be. I need my fur," I said.

"Don't worry. I'm sure she won't say anything rude to you."

But I wasn't even worried about that until my mom said it. As I walked through the parking lot, I was hoping that I could just look for Mrs. Potaski's head and avoid it. But that didn't happen. Because before I even got inside the store, I saw Mrs. Potaski.

"Holy crud! She's in the store window," I said. "Painting eyelashes!"

My mother and I froze in front of the store window. This was something that Mrs. Potaski did sometimes to drum up business for Country Buttons. She sat in the store window display at a small craft table and demonstrated how to paint eyelashes on ceramic doll heads. She looked so steady inside that window.

"I don't know how she does it," my mom said.

"I do. She's a frozen person," I said.

Right as I said that, Mrs. Potaski finished one doll head and picked up another one.

"She's a robot," I said.

"We need to stop staring at Mrs. Potaski and go buy your fur," my mother said.

"Right."

When we entered the craft store, I felt pretty thrilled. There was a whole corner dedicated to fake fur. There were so many colors that I could have been any color bear I wanted. I could have been some weird, rainbow, neon-colored bear. But I didn't want that. I wanted to be a grizzly bear and that meant brown fur.

"Can I help you?" a clerk asked us.

"Yes, my daughter is trying to make a grizzly bear costume."

The woman clapped her hands together. "Are you trying out for the mascot? I just helped another girl buy grizzly bear fur."

"What?" I asked, glancing around. "Who?" I couldn't believe that another person had an idea that was as good as mine.

"That young lady over there," the clerk said. "With the wrist brace."

I couldn't stop blinking. It was Alice Potgeiser. She was standing in line in the craft store buying yards and yards of fake brown fur. What was wrong with her? Did she want to be a cheerleader *and* a mascot? Jerk.

"It's okay," my mom said. "You knew other people were trying out."

I stomped my foot and huffed. "I didn't know Alice Potgeiser was trying out. She's already a cheerleader. She shouldn't be trying out. She's an expert gymnast. I can't believe this!"

"Well, it looks like she's injured her hand," my mom said. "Maybe she can't be a cheerleader this season."

"I don't care about her injury. She's rude."

"I didn't mean to start a ruckus," the clerk said. "I suggest that you select a fur that doesn't exceed a one-quarter-inch nap."

"What's a nap?" I asked.

"The nap is the length of the fur," the clerk explained.

"Oh, then we'll need a three- or four-inch nap. I'm supposed to be a bear," I said.

"Will you be sewing it? Because I always remind my customers to sew with the nap. Not against it."

My mother did not look thrilled to learn this. "We'll take three yards of this," she said, patting a furry brown fabric that I felt could have been furrier.

I watched Alice buy her fur and walk out of the store. "Looking like a bear was my great idea. It was going to be my secret weapon."

My mother carried the fur in her arms to the checkout stand. "Just because she dresses like a bear doesn't mean that she'll beat you."

"But she's an expert gymnast!" I whined.

"She won't be doing any tumbling with a wrist injury," my mom said. "You two are on an equal playing field."

This made me feel a lot better. "Yeah. In fact, her injury probably makes her a worse bear right out of the gate."

"I don't know that we need to put it that way," my mom said.

"Sure we do!" I said. Finally, my mom was thinking like

a winner and we were back on the same team. "I'm going to kick Alice Potgeiser's rude gymnastic butt."

"There's no need to get graphic," my mom said.

"I'm just keeping it real."

As we left the store, it was hard not to stop and stare some more at Mrs. Potaski. After she finished painting eyelashes on a doll head, she put it on the floor to dry. There were over two dozen heads spread out around her.

"She's a machine," I said.

"She's very talented," my mother added.

"Do you think she can hear us?" I asked.

And right when I asked that, Mrs. Potaski looked up at us. I felt a little strange. Because I hadn't seen her since she'd split up Sylvie and me in my living room. After she looked at us, Mrs. Potaski did something she rarely did. She smiled. And waved!

"She's smiling and waving!" I said.

"I know," my mom said.

"Hi, Mrs. Potaski!" I yelled at the window. "I miss seeing you! And Sylvie!" Even though I hated Sylvie for being a blabbermouth, I still missed her.

Then I saw Mrs. Potaski's lips move, but I couldn't hear what she was saying.

"What?" I shouted.

I saw her lips move some more.

"Speak up!" I yelled.

"She says you should stop by," my mom said.

I turned and looked at my mom in disbelief. "I didn't hear that."

"I read her lips," she said.

I didn't even know my mom could do that. I looked back at Mrs. Potaski and her lips moved again. So I tried to read them too. And it worked. "Holy crud! She did tell me to stop by.

"I'll stop by soon!" I yelled at the window. "Have a good day in there!"

Then Mrs. Potaski waved goodbye to me. And I waved goodbye to Mrs. Potaski. And my mom loaded my grizzly fur onto the backseat. I imagined how awesome my bear outfit was going to look. My heart thumped happily all the way home.

# CHAPTER

## 22

For some reason, my mom didn't want to make my bear outfit as soon as we got home. She didn't want to make it until the night before tryouts in front of the school, which I thought was lame. Because I still had another practice at school. And it would have been fun for me to practice in my bear outfit at home. But my mom said, "No way. I'll sew it for when you need it, not when you want it."

At dinner, my fur was the topic of the night. My dad seemed excited about it. "It's a great color. But what are you going to do for a head?" he asked.

"I'm going to use my own head. I might glue some fur to my face."

"You aren't gluing any fur to your face," my mom said. But I didn't know if that was true.

That night, I didn't have a single nightmare. And I also had a pretty good day at school the next day. In nutrition, I learned what a bioflavonoid was. But by the time school was over I'd forgotten what a bioflavonoid was. I wanted to get to mascot practice early, because I needed to secure a place in the front. Because last time I was in the back and I didn't have the best view of some of the hand and arm moves. Tragically, Dolan the Puker also wanted to be near the front. For some weird reason he also decided that he wanted to talk to me.

"I'm Dolan," he said. "I think we have gym at the same time."

I glared at Dolan a little bit. Because when he told me that it reminded me that he'd seen me doing downward-facing dog. "I'm Bessica."

"Why'd your parents name you that?" he asked.

I stretched my arms over my head to warm up my muscles and did some bending forward. "I'm named after the first woman in the United States to fly solo in a plane."

"I thought that was Amelia Earhart," Dolan said.

I shook my head. "She was the first woman to fly solo across the Atlantic Ocean." When I told people about my name, they often brought up Amelia Earhart, so I had to learn a little bit about her.

"What's your special talent going to be?" Dolan asked me.

I was already sick of talking to him. "I'm going to cheer like a bear mascot."

"Yeah, but at final mascot practice, everybody who tries out does a special talent. What's yours going to be?"

I didn't answer him. I kept glaring at him like maybe he was lying.

"I'm going to ride around the gym and show off my mad bicycle-racing skills. I brought my own bike."

I stopped stretching and looked at his bike leaning up against a wall. I didn't think he was lying anymore. "Nobody mentioned the special talent part to me."

"It's printed on the cheer page we got."

"No, it's not," I said. I dug through my backpack until I found my cheer page. There wasn't any such thing written on it.

"On the back," Dolan said.

I turned it over. But it was blank. "There's nothing on the back," I said.

"Sucks to be you. Looks like you got a bad cheer page," Dolan said. Then he smiled a little like a jerk.

"Do we have to do our talent today?" I asked.

"Yeah," he said. "That's how they determine the final three."

"Huh?" Nobody had mentioned a final three to me either.

"That information is on the back of the cheer sheet too."

I looked at Dolan's cheer sheet. Everything he'd mentioned was spelled out right there in black and white. Today was the day that we cheered in front of Ms. Rich and showed her our mascot talent. Based on the results, three people would be chosen to compete in front of the whole school.

"How did I miss this?" I asked.

"Beats me," he said. Then he walked off and started talking to Maddie Bell.

I couldn't believe it. I hadn't even made my bear costume yet and I might have already lost my chance to wear it. I glanced around. Alice was wearing a cool-looking fur outfit. It sucked. I should have been wearing my fur clothes too. I felt very defeated. So defeated that I left the gym and hurried into the hallway. And I pushed open the door so fast that it smashed into somebody who was carrying a soda can and knocked him down.

"Sorry," I said. Then I realized it was Blake and I felt a little bit extra sorry. Because in addition to his parents getting divorced and his getting shoved inside a trash can, he was on the ground with a soda spilled all over him because he'd been hit with a door.

"Ugh," he moaned.

"I hope you didn't break anything," I said. Then I picked up his backpack for him and held it until he got up.

"Where's my jump rope?" he asked.

I saw it. It had skittered across the floor. "It's over there."

Blake limped over and picked it up. Then he took his backpack from me. And I got a very good and creative idea.

"Can I borrow that?" I asked.

"No," Blake said. "I need my backpack."

"Your jump rope!" I said.

Blake looked at it and then at me. "I need it for PE. It's a doctor-approved alternative to lifting weights."

Poor Blake. He was much dweebier than I realized.

"I'll give it back to you tomorrow. I promise!"

I think Blake could tell that I was in a desperate situation. Because instead of telling me no again, he handed it to me.

"Thank you so much!" I said. Then I rushed into the gymnasium and sat down and visualized myself winning one of the three spots. It didn't matter that Dolan the Puker was going to show off his mad bicycle skills. Or that Alice Potgeiser had a fur outfit. I had a solution.

After all the aspiring mascots had gathered on the mat, Ms. Rich made the announcement that we had one more auditioner. And then she introduced Alice Potgeiser and I felt myself wanting to boo, but I didn't.

"I'm going to call you up one by one to demonstrate your cheer ability and your mascot talent."

It was just like Dolan the Puker said. I watched as people went up to the front one by one and yelled about how excited they were to beat the other team. There was a lot of roaring involved, and I wasn't sure why, because I thought that bears growled.

"Bessica Lefter," Ms. Rich called.

I walked to the front. I swung my arms a lot and yelled "F-I-G-H-T! F-I-G-H-T!" Then I felt like I was losing the crowd, so I yelled, "I'm a bear!" Also, I started jumping rope a few times. And I sort of ripped off what Dolan the Puker had said and I cheered, "Watch my mad jump-roping skills!" I jumped around the room. Everybody was laughing.

"Nice talent!" Ms. Rich said. "We've never had a mascot jump rope before."

I was so happy to hear that I didn't pay total attention when the other people went. Also, I got out my phone and texted Grandma. "I just tried out for mascot! And I make a great bear!" And Grandma must not have been in a cave because she texted me back, "Right on!"

After practice I felt a little nervous and unsure if I was good enough to win a spot or not. Because some of the people had cool talents. Maddie Bell played the flute. Alice Potgeiser, while in her fur suit, did amazing high kicks. And this one girl named Pia Jardin did magic and made a stuffed pigeon fly out of her backpack. It was cool.

When I walked out to the car I was exhausted.

"How did it go?" my mom asked.

"Tomorrow we find out if I made the final three," I said.

"Wow," my mom said. "I bet you did great."

That night I was really hoping to get a postcard from Grandma. But that didn't happen. And the next day, when I woke up, I felt so hot that I thought maybe our thermostat was broken. In fact, I didn't even get up.

"You're sick, Bessica," my mother said. "You need to stay home."

"But I find out if I'm a winner or a loser today. I've got to go!" I tried to get out of bed. But not very hard.

"I'll call the school and find out," my mom said.

"When you get home?" I asked. "I don't think I can wait that long."

My mom shook her head. "No, I'll call right now."

I couldn't believe that was even an option. I kept my head on my pillow as my mom called the school from my bedroom. She explained I was sick and that she wanted to get the results. When she smiled and pumped her fist over her head, I knew.

"Did they say who else won?" I asked.

My mother nodded.

"Tell me," I said. "I have to know."

My mother sat down next to me and put her hand on my forehead. "You have a little fever."

But I didn't care about my little fever. I cared about my mascot competition.

"Did Alice make it? Did the secretary say the name Alice Potgeiser?"

My mother took her hand off my forehead and petted my pixie. "Yes. But don't worry about that now."

I reached up and held my mother's hand. "Who else?" I had to know. I couldn't imagine staying home all day with a fever and not knowing.

"Dolan Burr," my mother said.

I tightened my grip on my mother's hand. "The puker."

"You feel like throwing up?" my mother asked. She touched my forehead again in a more concerned way.

I shook my head. "No. My stomach feels normal."

"Let me get you some Tylenol and some crackers and juice."

"Cool," I said as I closed my eyes. "I am so happy."

"I am so proud of you." My mother bent down and kissed my forehead. "Let me call work. I don't think I can get it off, but I can probably work a half day."

"Okay. When will you make me my fur pants?" I asked.

"I'll start on them when I get home."

Those were the sweetest words I'd heard in a long, long time. I felt so hot and tired. The world hummed around me. "Thank you. Thank you. Thank you," I said.

\* \* \*

I didn't even hear my mom come home. Hunger woke me around lunch. And then I heard a very happy sound: the quiet motor of the sewing machine whirring in the kitchen.

"Are you making my fur outfit?" I called.

My mother came into my room and brought me a glass of orange juice. "This fur is very hard to sew. We might need to use glue."

That didn't sound ideal. But I didn't have the strength to disagree. "Will we glue the fur to my real clothes?"

"I think so."

"Won't that ruin my real clothes?"

"Probably."

"Can you try to sew it again? I like my real clothes."

My mother set down the glass of orange juice and left the room. I heard the sewing machine whirring away. And then I fell asleep. And when I woke up, I was looking at an awesome pair of fur pants.

"Wow. Did you end up using glue?" I asked.

My mother shook her head. "I sewed them. It nearly killed me, but I did it."

"Cool," I said. "Where are my paws? And my fur top?"

My mother looked like she was on the verge of tears. "No top. No paws. Just pants."

I gasped a little, even though I was weak and that was hard to do. "But I need to look better than Alice Potgeiser."

"They're not going to vote for the person with the best

fur suit. They're going to vote for the person who's the best mascot."

It was official. My mother was no longer on my team. "They will vote for the best overall bear. If I only wear fur pants, then I'm not an overall bear. I'm just a half-bear."

My mother groaned. "You're going to have to make it work."

"But I'm sick. You shouldn't grouch at me when I'm ill," I pleaded.

"You're right. I'm taking a lunch break."

And I didn't see my mom again until I woke up all sweaty and tired, in time for dinner.

"Mom! Mom!" I called. But she didn't come. I thought about yelling for her again, but then I decided to call Grandma. Because every time I'd gotten sick while Grandma lived here, she'd brought me movies to keep me from getting bored and ginger ale to settle my stomach. I wished I had those things now.

> **Me:** (*cough*) Grandma, I am very sick.
>
> **Grandma:** Sweetheart, I'm sorry to hear that, but I can't talk right now.
>
> **Me:** But I'm very sick.
>
> **Grandma:** I'm in the hospital.
>
> **Me:** (*gasp*) Are you dying? Should we come right away?

**Grandma:** It's Willy.

**Me:** Wow. That's too bad that Willy's dying.

**Grandma:** He's not dying. He got injured. He fell.

**Me:** Off of something?

**Grandma:** Yes. A small mountain.

**Me:** Uh-oh! Did he break his neck?

**Grandma:** I don't think he broke anything. But a tumble like that at our age is a serious thing. Can I call you later, doll?

**Me:** I guess.

Hearing about Willy made me feel a little bit guilty. Because for weeks I'd been visualizing him falling off a mountain. Grandma sounded so sad and worried. Maybe it was my low-grade fever or maybe it was my conscience, but that moment I knew that it was wrong to mess with somebody's E-Date Me Today account. And it was also wrong to mess with the hearts of all of Grandma's potential boyfriends. So I went downstairs, and pulled the plug on my great idea. I opened up her account.

So many wonderful men wanted to meet for sandwiches. I wished that Grandma could have given them a chance.

And I couldn't stop myself from checking out the picture of the SS *Funshine* again. It was so beautiful.

I felt awful when I saw that Pilot Mike had written back to Grandma. In fact, I felt so bad that I opened the email in an attempt to make myself feel better. Because maybe Pilot Mike hadn't even agreed to meet Grandma.

> Rhoda, this all sounds wonder-
> ful. Give me a call at your con-
> venience and we'll set it up.
> (406) 234-0623. Can't wait to
> take you waterskiing! Mike

When I read Pilot Mike's email I almost died. Because I was staring at the biggest coincidence ever. His phone number was exactly the same as my locker combination. Twice! I blinked at it several times. Then I heard myself say, "Holy crud!" It was like I'd found the perfect person for Grandma, but because Grandma had a maniac welder boyfriend who'd fallen off a mountain, now she and perfect Pilot Mike would never meet.

Once, last year, I watched a movie on cable with my mom that was a little bit like this. My mom went through an entire box of tissues, and at the end, in a weepy voice, she called what we'd seen a "terrible romantic tragedy." I couldn't believe Grandma and Pilot Mike were having one of those. But they were. And I couldn't believe I was responsible for it. But I was.

As hard as it was, I knew what I needed to do. *Click. Click. Click.* It was so sad sending Pilot Mike back into the trash bin. His deleted message was the saddest thing I'd looked at in a long time. I thought of all the fun Grandma and I weren't going to have aboard the SS *Funshine*. That, too, was a terrible tragedy. *Click. Click. Click.*

# CHAPTER

23

I really wanted to practice being a mascot in my fur pants, but Mom kept saying that I had to rest. But I didn't want to rest anymore. I was feeling better. Tryouts were tomorrow. It made sense that I should practice wearing my fur pants.

Even though my mom wouldn't let me help her, I stood in the yard Sunday afternoon while she cleared it. My dad was going to mow for the final time before fall and the first hard frost.

"You want to make sure that you're fully recovered," my mom said, handing me my Frisbee.

"I know," I said.

When my dad came out to mow the lawn, I was horrified to see that he was wearing shorts.

"Why is he wearing shorts?" I asked. "His skin is pasty white!"

"Shhh," my mother said. "It's a hot day. Give him a break."

I watched his pasty white legs as he walked the yard's perimeter. He didn't totally trust my mom and me to clear the lawn one hundred percent, because over the summer he'd hit a few things that we'd overlooked: our thesauruses, a sprinkler head, and two cupcake pans.

"Looks good!" he said. He wiped some sweat off his face. "I might need to change into my tank top."

I looked in horror at my mother.

"It's hot, Bessica," my mother said.

"But we live in civilization," I said. "That means adults wear clothes. Even while doing yard work!"

I hadn't realized I was yelling, but I was.

"Don't yell at your father," my mother said.

"I wasn't!" I yelled.

"Bessica, I think you need to go to your room and rest."

"I think you're right!" Then I stomped off. Because sitting in my room and recovering was a whole lot better than watching my dad ride around our yard on the lawn mower, showing the world his pasty white legs.

Lying down on top of my bed, I found it hard not to cry. But I wasn't sure why I felt like crying. Was it because Sylvie had become a fake person and decided to become Malory's friend and not mine? Was it because Grandma had become a crazy person and abandoned me? Was it because I had lost my chance to board the SS *Funshine*? Was it because middle school was terrible? Was it because I didn't have any friends yet? Was it because I was worried I wasn't going to win the mascot contest? Which one was it?

My door squeaked open.

"Hi, sunshine," my mom said.

But when my mom said the word *sunshine* it made me think of the SS *Funshine*, and that made me feel terrible.

"What are you thinking about?"

And I didn't lie. "A yacht."

My mother sat down next to me. "You're thinking about a yacht, and that's making you cry?"

I sniffled. "Yeah. I really like water sports." I sniffled more. "Do you know who else really likes water sports?"

"Who?" my mother asked, rubbing my back.

"Grandma." My voice broke when I said her name.

"Bessica, she'll be home in less than three weeks."

"But she's going to miss my mascot tryouts and she'll be coming back with Willy. I'm not an idiot. Things will be different. They'll probably rent another stupid Winnebago and go on another stupid trip. There are a lot of caves in the world. I know. I looked on the Internet."

"Sunshine, you had your grandma all to yourself for a lot of years. You have a bunch of great memories."

When I heard this I burst into tears. Because I remembered a part in my collaborative diary where I'd written about all the rides I'd ridden on with Grandma at the Eastern Idaho State Fair, which included the Flying Saucer, and I wished I had those pages, just like Sylvie had her ocean pictures.

"Sometimes things happen in life that we don't want and we have to adapt. Look at poor Betty with her mallet toe and infection. That's rough. But she's bouncing back."

I looked at my mom and studied her face. "Are you comparing my life to mallet-toe Betty's life? That's mean."

"Let's talk when you feel better," my mom said.

But I didn't think I was still sick. I felt like I was fully recovered.

"Can I at least touch my fur pants?" I asked.

My mom carried them over from where they were hanging on the door and placed them at the foot of the bed. "They're wonderful," I said. "But how will I keep them from falling down?" Because they didn't have a zipper. And I'd never worn a pair of pants that didn't.

"You'll wear suspenders," my mom said.

"Cool," I said. I'd never worn suspenders before. And then I put my head on my pillow and zonked out.

I might have stayed zonked out all night, but I didn't. Because I heard the sound of a bedroom intruder. I opened my eyes very quickly and yelled, "Get out!" But then I saw my dad standing next to me holding my bear pants.

"These look great," he said.

"Thanks. You can stay."

"Blake stopped by to pick up his jump rope."

I grabbed my heart and made a gasping sound. I needed that jump rope. "Did you tell him to go away?"

"I gave it to him. But don't worry, sunshine. Your mom went and bought you a new one that's identical to his."

I let out a very relieved breath. I thought my dad's story about Blake should have started with that information.

He sat down next to me. "I've been thinking about something."

"Oh," I said. I hoped it wasn't related to the mean things I'd yelled about his pasty white legs. Because I felt bad about that.

"It's about your bear costume. I think you're missing something."

When I heard this, I sat up a little. Because I loved my fur pants, but I definitely thought my costume was still missing important bear parts.

"Hind paws," he said.

Then he held up a pair of my old sneakers. And this bummed me out. Because I didn't want to wear those ever again. They smelled bad. I was surprised they weren't in a garbage can somewhere.

"I don't even want to be in the same room with those things." I plopped my head down again.

"But look!" he said. Then he showed me a bunch of fur pieces. "They're scraps from your pants."

"Ooh!" I said. I thought maybe I could stick with my original idea and glue some fur pieces to my face.

"If we glue them to your shoes, you'll have terrific hind paws." My dad lifted my smelly shoes up in the air again.

Even though my shoes smelled, this was such a good idea that I couldn't object. So my dad went and got several sheets of newspaper and we spread them out on my bedroom floor, and for the next hour my dad and I glued fur pieces to my shoes. He wanted to use all-purpose craft glue, but I insisted that we use superglue. Because I felt that if the word *super* was in the name, it was the best possible choice.

When we were done, my father lifted the shoes up and whistled. "We'll have to put these in the garage so you don't inhale glue fumes all night."

"Good," I said. While they weren't as bad as hummus sandwich fumes, I didn't particularly enjoy inhaling glue fumes either.

Before my dad could leave with my shoes, my cell phone started ringing.

"It's late," he said. "Who's calling you?" But I shrugged, because I didn't even know who would be calling me. Then I looked at my phone and saw that it was Vicki.

"It's Vicki Docker!" I said. "She's in high school."

My dad stood right there while I took the call.

**Vicki:** I'm calling to wish you good luck.

**Me:** Oh my heck. Thanks for remembering!

**Vicki:** Do you have any final questions?

**Me:** I'm not sure.

**Vicki:** Make sure you drink plenty of fluids so you don't overheat.

**Me:** Thanks. I'll be wearing fur pants, so that might happen.

**Vicki:** Fur pants? Really? Uh-oh.

**Me:** Why are you saying "uh-oh"?

**Vicki:** Have you thought about thigh chafe?

**Me:** No.

**Vicki:** You should think about it. Your fur-textured pants could create intense skin friction. And intense skin friction can cause chafing. And chafing can cause a rash. And a rash can cause weeks of thigh discomfort. And you don't want that. I speak from experience. Do you own any long underwear?

**Me:** Possibly. I think they violate a decency rule.

**Vicki:** I strongly urge you to wear them. For long-term mascot success, avoiding rashes is essential.

**Me:** Right.

**Vicki:** Remember, the winner will be the one who brings the most intensity. Knock 'em out, Bessica.

**Me:** Okay. I'll bring it.

After I hung up, my dad looked at me like he wanted me to tell him what that was all about. But I didn't want to do that, because I didn't want to say words like *thigh chafe* and *long underwear* in front of him. Because he was my dad.

"Well, it looks like it's time for bed," he said, walking toward my door.

"It does look like that," I said.

He smiled at me. And it reminded me of something I needed to say.

"Dad, I'm sorry that I said unkind things about your white legs today. I love you. And I really appreciate that you mow the lawn every week, even when it's hot."

"Thanks." His smile got bigger. "I like mowing the lawn. And I love you too. Maybe next summer I'll work on tanning my legs. Maybe we can go to Bear Lake or Cub River and get tanned together."

"Maybe," I said. But by then I'd be a seventh grader, and I wasn't sure if seventh graders tanned their legs with their dads. Then he shut the door, and I zonked out all over again.

# CHAPTER 24

I woke up Monday feeling fully recovered. Except I was worried about one thing. How was I going to get my bear pants to school? My mom solved this dilemma by offering to drive me.

"You're going to be great," she said as she pulled into the parking lot.

"If I lose, this is going to be the second-saddest day of my life." I didn't bother telling her what the saddest day of my life was, because I figured she already knew. It was the day I lost Sylvie and Grandma.

We were going to hold the assembly after lunch. This

was good because it gave me plenty of time to put on my fur pants and get used to my suspenders by walking around the gym. Alice was there too, with her fur suit. And she was talking on the phone, complaining that she needed her bear head. After she hung up I asked her the obvious question.

"You have a bear head?"

"Yeah. My mom bought it for me. It's on its way."

That bummed me out. Because I'd given up on the idea of making a bear head and just planned on using my own head. Watching Alice walk around, I couldn't believe that Sylvie had ever shown her our diary. So, like a very mature person, I asked her about it.

"Have you read my diary?"

Alice looked at me like I was a freak. "How would I do that?"

"I'm just thinking about what you said to me in the office."

"Oh, about Kettle Harris. We're cousins. A couple of years ago he brought a bunch of letters you'd written to him to a family reunion."

"What?" I asked. I'd forgotten I'd written those letters. I couldn't even remember what I'd said in them.

"Yeah, your 'crush letters.' You sent him, like, twenty notes telling him that you liked him."

"He took those to your family reunion?" I'd been to a couple of family reunions and we'd never done anything like that.

"I don't really have time to talk about this. I need to stay focused for my tumbling."

"What?" I asked. I felt doomed. "How can you tumble with a wrist brace?"

"I'll be doing one-armed flips," she said. "You know what they say about mascots. You've got to bring it."

I felt sick to my stomach. When the assembly finally started, the three of us stood off to the side of the gym: Alice Potgeiser, Dolan the Puker, and me. It was so stressful. One of us would be the mascot. One of us would spend the next nine months of our lives dressed as a bear, cheering on our athletic teams. Looking out into the crowd of middle-school-student faces and teacher faces, I had never wanted anything more in my life.

I stood between Alice and Dolan in my furry pants and suspenders and fur-covered shoes. The fur was peeling off my sneakers a little bit, but I tried not to pay attention to that. Any moment, the whistle would sound and we'd each have two minutes to do our cheers. Alice was a lot furrier than I was. Plus, her mother was bringing her a bear head, but no such thing had happened yet. I had my doubts that the bear head even existed.

Alice was up first, which was good and bad. Good: I

didn't have to go first. Also, it gave her mom less time to arrive with the *alleged* bear head. Bad: I would have to follow her and possibly feel intimidated by any flips she'd done. Dolan would go last, which I suspected was assigned to him based on his puking history. Principal Tidge was very practical, and if Dolan made a mess of the floor, better that nobody had to go after him.

"Alice Potgeiser!" cheered Principal Tidge. Then the whistle blew and Alice and her fluffy hair were off. She ran and jumped up and immediately kicked her legs apart and performed a series of airborne splits. She looked exactly like a cheerleader. Sure, she had school spirit. But there was nothing mascot-y about what she was doing. I didn't understand her logic. If she kept this up, I knew she was going to lose. It was thrilling. Then I saw a woman rush onto the gym floor. And she was carrying something hairy. Uh-oh. It was a bear head! I couldn't believe my eyes.

The woman handed the furry head to Alice and she slipped it over her fluffy head. And then she started dancing in a way that had a ton of butt wiggling. And everybody started laughing. And she waved to people. And danced. And then she did something that I thought was impossible. While wearing the bear head, Alice Potgeiser performed a dozen one-armed flips. One after the other. It was disgusting. Because it looked totally awesome and the bear head stayed on the whole time. I looked at Dolan.

"*I* feel like puking," I whispered to him. But he didn't say anything back. When Alice was finished, the entire audience erupted in applause. It sounded like happy thunder. It was terrible. Alice trotted back over to the line and looked at me and said, "Good luck!"

But I knew she didn't mean it. I watched her take her bear head off. Her face looked sweaty, red, and hot. I held my jump rope and wished for the best. Then it happened. "Bessica Lefter!" Principal Tidge called. And the whistle blew.

I ran out in front of everybody waving my arms, so they would understand that I was full of energy. Then I hopped around and yelled, "Go bears! Go bears! Go bears!" While I hopped, I realized that wearing "underneath pants" and tights to prevent chafing under my fur pants was a bad idea. Because I was getting pretty hot. But there wasn't much I could do about it now. So I started my cheer.

"What do we eat? What do we eat? Tiger meat! Tiger meat! How do we like it? How do we like it? Raw! Raw! Raw!" People cheered. Apparently, they liked the idea of a bear eating a tiger raw. So I launched into my laughter-grabbing routine. I swung my rope over my head and started jumping. And I didn't stand in one place like I was lazy. I took off and jumped around the whole gym. And while I jumped I kept cheering, "Go bears! Go bears! Go bears!"

And as I was doing this, I got so hot I started to sweat. A lot. I could feel it running down my back. And my face. I actually saw some drops splatter onto the gym's wood floor. But I was afraid to stop. Because Vicki said that the winner would be the person who brought the most intensity. So I kept jumping. Even when my time was over. I headed back toward my line, but I didn't stop jumping rope. And people noticed this and kept cheering, so I decided to yell more crazy, clever stuff.

"Bring me a tiger! I'll eat it! Raw! Raw! Raw!" And then I did a bunch of growling. And Dolan the Puker looked at me like he was ready to begin his mascot cheer, but I didn't care. Because I was still bringing it. In fact, I felt so good about how things were going that I started jump roping around the gym again, even though it was probably against the rules. People laughed their heads off. Normally, this would have really bothered me, but because I was wearing fur pants, I didn't take their laughter personally.

*Jump. Jump. Jump.* I was so hot I was practically panting. I could feel my feet sweating inside my shoes. And that was when it happened. I felt my first shoe fly off. And then my second. But it wasn't a totally bad thing, because it cooled off my toes. I watched them lying on the gym floor. Huge fur chunks had fallen off. I guess the glue I used wasn't as super as I'd thought.

And even though I was wearing socks, I didn't stop

jumping. In fact, I didn't even mess up. I was so proud of myself. I felt like I'd already won mascot. And that was when everything fell apart. I saw something huge and brown fly through the air. And at the same time, I suddenly felt a lot less hot. Then I realized what had happened. I heard my suspenders clatter to the floor. I'd lost my pants! And because they'd come off and gotten caught in my jump rope, I'd accidentally flung them into the audience. I stopped jumping rope and looked out into the crowd to see where they'd gone. It didn't take me long to spot them. They were on top of Ms. Penrod's head. I'd flung my fur pants onto a former Olympian! Everybody was laughing. Even Alice Potgeiser. Even Principal Tidge. I wasn't sure how to feel about this.

I reached down to pick up my jump rope. That was when I heard somebody yell, "Look at her butt!" Then I remembered what I was wearing. My purple pants with KISS THIS written across the butt. I wanted to die. No, that's not true. I wanted to pretend like this had never happened and then I wanted to die in ninety years, at the end of my life. I didn't even want to be the mascot anymore. I wanted to erase this moment. I walked back to the line.

"I can't believe it," Alice said. "You did a great job. I mean, you were hilarious."

But I don't think she meant that as a compliment. I looked out into the laughing crowd. Even rude Raya Papas looked like she was laughing. I shut my eyes. I was so relieved when I heard Principal Tidge announce that it was Dolan the Puker's turn. Only she didn't call him Dolan the Puker. She just called him Dolan Burr.

I stood very still in my purple KISS THIS pants next to Alice Potgeiser while Dolan the Puker rode around on a tricycle wearing a triangular fur hat.

"Where's his bicycle?" I asked.

"It got stolen," Alice said. And the way she said this made me wonder whether she had anything to do with it.

"That's a weird hat," I said.

"It looks like a beaver, not a bear," Alice said.

Dolan didn't yell crazy, clever things. And he didn't bring intensity either. He just rode around on that tricycle like a madman, yelling, "I'm a bear! I'm a bear!"

It was lame.

Even though I was totally humiliated, and had basically sweat my pants off in front of the entire school, I was pretty sure I'd done a better job than Dolan the Puker. I glanced at Alice. She watched him in a very focused way. Then, when he parked his tricycle, she glanced at me.

"Sweating your pants off and flinging them onto the PE teacher was totally desperate," she said. "I didn't realize you played hardball."

I looked Alice Potgeiser right in the eye. She was acting like a total psycho-bully and I was sick of it.

I pointed at myself and said, "I bring it."

And then Alice Potgeiser didn't look at me or talk to me for the rest of the assembly. People clapped for Dolan, but not as hard as they'd clapped for me. He returned to the line and stood next to me. On top of his sweaty head, his triangle fur hat smelled like wet dog.

"That was a lot of fun!" Principal Tidge said, like she was trying to reassure us. "You have until the end of the day to cast your ballot for one of our three mascots. And Friday we'll have another assembly and I'll announce the results."

There was a bunch of cheering after she said this, but I think it was because people wanted to get out of class for another assembly. Didn't they understand the importance of school spirit? As people poured out of the gym, my heart felt like it was going to explode. I was both excited and depressed. Because I wanted to be a mascot, but I wasn't ready to humiliate myself on a regular basis. I wondered what my chances were. I wondered how many people at my school would vote for the girl who'd lost her pants.

# CHAPTER

I t turns out that a lot of people wanted to vote for the girl who lost her pants. As I was leaving school that day, people kept yelling, "You've got my vote!" And I didn't even know who these people were. I guess Vicki was right. It's important to take risks. It's important to show up, be proud, and shake your rear end like a wild animal.

As I walked to the bus, there was one person I wanted to call more than anybody. But Sylvie was at school. So I got on my bus and rode home and sat on top of all my excitement. And when I got home I had to sit on it even longer, because my mom's car had broken down and my dad had to go and pick her up.

Waiting was hard. I took my carefully folded fur pants and set them on my bed. Then I bounced around the house from room to room. Then I realized that I was in such a wonderful mood that I was pretty sure Grandma would want to hear from me. So I called her.

> **Me:** I just tried out for mascot, and while things didn't go exactly how I wanted them to go, I think I have a shot.
>
> **Grandma:** I don't doubt that.
>
> **Me:** Grandma, I haven't told anybody this, but if I don't win, I will have to live in loner town for the next three years.
>
> **Grandma:** Bessica, you'll only live in loner town if you choose to live in loner town.
>
> **Me:** That's not true, Grandma. That might be how things work in caves, but that's not how things work in middle school. Hey, is that Willy in the background?
>
> **Grandma:** Yes. He needs a pillow.

**Me:** So he's gonna live?

**Grandma:** Of course he is. Willy has endurance!

**Me:** Oh. Grandma, I need to apologize for two things.

**Grandma:** Okay.

**Me:** First, I'm sorry that I've been unkind to Willy. He's nice to me. From now on I'll be nice too.

**Grandma:** It's good to hear you say that.

**Me:** Second, I created a terrible romantic tragedy.

**Grandma:** Is this about Noll Beck?

**Me:** No. It's about you and Pilot Mike. I set up a date for you guys, because you both like sandwiches and waterskiing. His phone number is (406) 234-0623. Maybe you could call him and let him down easy.

**Grandma:** What?

**Me:** He has a boat. I thought you'd really like him.

**Grandma:** Bessica! How did you meet a pilot with a boat? Did he visit your school for career day or something?

**Me:** No. Not quite. He lives in Montana.

**Grandma:** I don't have time for you to explain this to me. Willy needs me.

**Me:** That's cool. I understand that.

**Grandma:** Bessica, you should not have set me up.

**Me:** I know. I regret that I did that. It's why I'm apologizing.

**Grandma:** What's his number again?

**Me:** It's (406) 234-0623. It's identical to my locker combination. Twice.

**Grandma:** I'm going to tell him the truth.

**Me:** Okay. Grandma?

**Grandma:** Yes.

**Me:** I suddenly got very scared that I'm going to lose. The kids at my school vote for the winner and nobody really knows me.

**Grandma:** Don't fret yourself into despair. Being the front-runner isn't always the safest position. People love a good underdog story.

**Me:** That's exactly what I needed to hear.

**Grandma:** Good. I've got to go, doll.

**Me:** Are you mad at me about Pilot Mike?

**Grandma:** I'm not happy about it, but I know you didn't mean to hurt anybody.

**Me:** That's true.

**Grandma:** Bye for now. I've got my fingers crossed.

When my mom and dad pulled up in the driveway, I was watching through the window. As soon as they came through the door, they wanted a play-by-play of how things went. So I told them all about Alice and the bear head.

"A girl's mother purchased a bear head for her?" my mom asked.

"Yeah," I said. "It was totally furry."

My dad whistled. "Sounds like somebody has money to burn."

My dad loved to use that phrase when he thought rich people were buying stupid things.

"It even had fangs," I said.

"Bears don't have fangs," my dad said. "They have pronounced eyeteeth."

I blinked. I didn't see much of a difference.

Then I told them about Dolan the Puker and his tricycle ride and smelly fur hat.

"Why are you calling him Dolan the Puker?" my mom asked.

And I didn't even realize I'd called him that.

"He's puked twice in chorus. On the people in the row in front of him. He's got a reputation."

My dad whistled again. "With a condition like that, you'd think he'd get put in the front."

I shook my head. "That wouldn't work. He's very tall."

"How did your performance go? Did they like watching a jump-roping bear?"

I didn't really want to tell my parents that I'd sweat my pants off, but I also didn't want to lie. So I told them everything, exactly how it had happened. My mother looked horrified. But my dad laughed.

"They just flew right off?" he asked.

"Yep. They were basically on Ms. Penrod's head before I could stop jumping rope."

"Amazing," my dad said, smiling.

"And then people read my butt and laughed harder," I said.

"Your butt?" my dad asked.

My mother put her head in her hands. "She was wearing pajama bottoms that said *Kiss this* on the rear."

"I don't think I've seen those pajama bottoms," my dad said.

"They're purple," I said. "Grandma sent them to me from South Dakota."

"Wow," my dad said. "You might win."

"Maybe," I said.

"Even if you don't win, you can try out again next year. Usually the older kids win, Buck," my mom said.

"Sometimes they don't," my dad said.

And this made me smile. Because it felt good to have my dad believe in me, even though I wasn't an older kid.

That night, after dinner, I really wanted to call Sylvie. But instead of doing that, I just stared at my phone. And then the best thing in the world happened. She called me!

"Bessica!" Sylvie said. "Everybody at my school is talking about you!"

"Really?" I said. It felt weird to hear that.

"You pulled your pants off and threw them on a teacher's head?"

"Sort of," I said.

"Unbelievable," Sylvie said. "I didn't know that you had that in you."

"Well, when it comes to winning mascot, there are three things you've got to do. Thing one: Show up. Thing two: Be proud. Thing three: Shake your rear end like a wild animal!"

"You're so funny," Sylvie said. "I forgot how funny you are."

"Yeah. I'm pretty funny."

"Bessica, I miss you," Sylvie said.

And my heart sped up. Hearing Sylvie say those words was the sweetest moment of my year.

"I miss you too," I said.

"We should hang out," Sylvie said.

"I know. I know. Your mom told me I could come over!"

"She's softening," Sylvie said.

"That's great!" I said. Mrs. Potaski needed some softening.

"She thinks you're becoming more mature."

"She does?" Because I didn't think I was becoming more mature. Then I added, "Don't tell her that I sweat off my pants."

"She told me we could hang out on Saturday if you're free."

I was so happy. I could feel a humming sensation dancing through me.

"I can show you my mascot moves!" I said.

"Yeah!" Sylvie said. "I've learned all kinds of dance stuff that would work really well for bears."

"Oh my heck!" I said. "That's so cool!"

"And maybe Malory can come!"

I stopped breathing.

"Bessica, you need to get to know Malory and forgive her for being a blabbermouth," Sylvie said.

I continued not breathing.

"I forgave you for yelling at me and accusing me of all sorts of terrible things that I didn't do and for telling me to get a terrible pixie cut."

I hated it when Sylvie got reasonable. I *had* yelled at her and accused her of things she hadn't done. So I cleared my throat and said Sylvie's name in a very serious way. "Sylvie Potaski."

"What?" she asked.

"I apologize for yelling at you and accusing you of showing people our diary."

"I never showed anybody," Sylvie said.

"I know." Then I tried to make it seem like no big deal. So I laughed and said, "It was a big misunderstanding. Ha-ha-ha."

"What? You need to explain," Sylvie said in an unhappy tone.

I felt so lame telling her the whole story. "She never read the diary. I sort of forgot that in third grade I wrote Kettle a few notes where I confessed my huge crush on him. And I guess he held on to them. And passed them around at a family reunion."

Sylvie gasped.

"Turns out he and Alice Potgeiser are second cousins."

"What a dweeb. Who takes notes like that to a family reunion?"

"Exactly," I said.

"Let's forget Kettle Harris and Alice Potgeiser."

"Totally," I said. Even though I was thinking about Alice quite a bit because I was really hoping I'd kicked her butt.

"Oh, Bessica, come over Saturday. I'll tell Malory to bring her ferret named Taco. He's amazing."

The thought of playing with Malory's ferret made me feel skittish.

"Why can't you give Malory a second chance?" Sylvie asked. "She's a nice person. She's trying to start over and be brand new. You of all people should understand that."

And when Sylvie put it that way, it made it hard for me to object.

"Okay," I said. "I'll come hang out with you and Malory, and play with Taco."

"Cool!" Sylvie said. And she sounded so happy. She sounded exactly like the old Sylvie I loved and missed.

"You've got to call me as soon as you know if you've won," Sylvie said.

"Okay," I said.

After I got ready for bed, I climbed under the covers and stared at my ceiling. I didn't think I'd be able to sleep at all. My mom cracked open the door and whispered to me.

"Have you called Grandma and told her how things went?"

"I did. She feels like I've got a shot. Because the world likes underdogs."

"That's true. But it's okay if you don't win too. It's not a matter of life or death."

"Sure it's not," I said.

Then my mom shut my door and left me in a huge cube of darkness. It was so hard to fall asleep. I thought it was never going to happen.

# CHAPTER

## 26

I wasn't sure how or when I would find out who won. I walked into school with my stomach tied in knots. Lots of people waved to me and said, "Great job!" But these people could have thought that I'd done a great job and then voted for Alice or Dolan the Puker.

Psycho-bully Redge glared at me like normal in nutrition. I got him his pen and sat very still while Mrs. Mounds took roll. Maybe I'd find out at lunch. Maybe I'd find out at the end of the day. Maybe they'd call me at home after school. Then the intercom in the room crackled to life. "Bessica Lefter, Dolan Burr, and Alice Potgeiser, please come to the office."

Holy crud! I was going to find out right now. Was I ready to find out right now? I stood up. Either I'd won and would secure a place in middle school as the awesome grizzly-bear mascot, or I'd lost and would go back to my old place, which wasn't anything.

"Good luck, Bessica," Mrs. Mounds said as I left the room.

"Thanks," I said.

Halfway to the office, I ran into Alice. "You look so freaked out," she said. And she didn't give me time to rebut this. She just kept talking. "You must feel rotten. I mean, this whole voting system is totally unfair to you. Seriously. I'm popular. I've been a cheerleader for a year and have tons of friends. Plus, I've got an injury, which pulls in a ton of sympathy votes. It's sort of impossible to beat me. So don't be supersad when you lose. Okay?"

I really wished I hadn't run into Alice. She was such a snobby downer. I couldn't believe she had such a huge group of friends. It was weird. When we got to the principal's office, Dolan the Puker was already seated in a chair in front of Principal Tidge's desk. I sat down on one side of him and Alice sat down on the other. She looked very confident. Dolan looked sort of like me: worried.

"Congratulations," Principal Tidge said. "All three of you did a spectacular job. Honestly, I'm sure you'd all make outstanding mascots for North Teton Middle School."

While that was a nice thing to say, I also knew that it

wasn't going to happen. I glanced at a pile of papers stuffed inside a box on top of a filing cabinet. There were so many that they were flowing out of the box and onto the floor. They were the ballots. Oh my heck! I could see my name checkmarked on some of them!

"Dolan," Principal Tidge said, "even though the votes were close, I am afraid that you did not win mascot. But nice job on that tricycle. You've got a great, creative future ahead of you."

Dolan stood up and left without saying anything. I looked at Alice. But Alice didn't look at me. I didn't like that we were being dismissed one person at a time. I felt Principal Tidge should have just announced the winner and gotten it over with.

"Bessica," she said.

I dropped my head a little bit in disappointment. I really thought I had a chance. In my heart I knew I would have made an awesome bear.

"Your mascot abilities are obviously innate. Your comedic timing is brilliant. Your sense of showmanship is a thrill to watch." She smiled at me so proudly. It was the way my parents smiled at me when I graduated from elementary school. I couldn't believe that she was about to tell me that I'd lost.

"Alice, you are one of the most acrobatically talented

people I have ever met. It is a joy to watch your strength and flexibility in action."

Alice beamed when Principal Tidge told her this.

"As impossible as this might seem"—she leaned forward on her desk—"there is no clear winner. It is a statistical tie."

"What?" Alice said. "That's impossible. Have all the ballots been counted?"

"Counted and recounted and recounted," Principal Tidge said.

"Does the whole school have to vote again?" I asked. That seemed like a huge waste of paper. Also, waiting for the results a second time would probably kill me.

"We have options," Principal Tidge said. "And what I've chosen to do is to split mascot duties evenly."

"What?" Alice asked. "There'll be two of us?"

Principal Tidge nodded. "Exactly. We'll take a schedule of the games and you two will decide who will cheer at which event. There are an even number of games. So you will divide them equally."

I couldn't believe there was a tie. I was going to be the mascot. Only half of the time. But that wasn't losing. That was half winning!

"There's got to be another solution," Alice said. "People were absent yesterday. They should have a chance to vote. They could cast the tie-breaking ballots!"

That made sense. I hoped Principal Tidge didn't do that. Because I'd rather be a half winner than a full loser.

"I don't mind being a half mascot," I said.

"You're a full mascot," Principal Tidge said. "Just half of the time."

I smiled. I looked at Alice. She wasn't smiling. She looked majorly upset.

"When will we divide out the games?" I asked. I thought of the various schools we played against. Would I fight the Snake River Tiger? Would I cheer against the Flat Creek Bald Eagle? Who would fight the Teton Village Cougar? And the Powderhorn Spud? I couldn't wait to find out.

"I've printed out schedules to send home with you so you can discuss it with your parents. Mrs. Batts will be in touch with them and then we'll generate a schedule."

"Who gets the costume? Normally the mascot gets to take it home," Alice said.

Principal Tidge nodded to a coatrack. There hung the giant fur costume. It looked like a real bear. Brown furry legs. Brown furry arms. And an enormous brown furry head. It looked awesome!

"We'll store it here, but you'll be able to check it out the day before games."

Alice released a puff of disappointment. "I think we should revote. This is insanity."

"The decision has been made," Principal Tidge said. "Congratulations to you both."

I stood up and looked at the toppling pile of votes again. It seemed impossible that there was an exact tie. But I guessed that anything was possible.

"I'm telling you right now that I want to fight the Buffalo Valley Wildcat," Alice said. "I hate Mikey Mason. He's the wildcat this year. I'll tear him down."

"Okay," I said.

"This is so ridiculous. Stupid wrist." She lifted her wrist brace and shook it at the ceiling. "Who are we kidding? Being a mascot is beneath me. I should be a cheerleader."

"You could always quit," I said. I thought this was a brilliant suggestion on my part.

"Dream on," Alice said. "Potgeisers don't quit. We conquer."

Then I decided to be the bigger person. "I know you're disappointed, but congratulations."

Alice looked at me in total disgust and blinked. "I can't believe you just said that. For a sixth grader, you are so sarcastic. Seriously. And who even votes for a sixth grader? Who?"

And I felt like telling her that I was not being sarcastic and about half of the school voted for a sixth grader. But I didn't. It was a no-win situation for me. If Alice wanted to be a jerk about half winning, I was just going to have to let her be a jerk. I kept walking back to nutrition. But before I went inside I decided to do something. I went to my locker and got out my banned cell phone. I looked left and right to make sure that nobody was watching. The coast was clear. So I texted Grandma:

> You were right. The world loves
> underdogs. I half won! Have fun
> with Willy. Come home soon.
> XXOO BL

# CHAPTER 27

My mom drove me to Sylvie's house for lunch on Saturday. In addition to my fur pants, I carried a box from the bakery that held four blueberry tarts. One tart for everybody.

"I don't even know if they'll like tarts," I said. "I should have brought cake. Everybody likes cake."

"Tarts are special. They'll be a huge hit!" my mom said as she pulled into Sylvie's driveway.

"I guess," I said. I couldn't remember ever eating a tart before. I balanced the box on my legs and carefully opened the car door.

"Do you want me to help you carry anything?"

I shook my head. I didn't need help.

"Are you sure you need to take your pants?" she asked.

My jaw dropped. "Of course I need to bring them. Sylvie is going to teach me dance moves. I need to learn how to do them in fur pants to make sure I do them properly."

My mom smiled. "I'm very proud of you. You're thinking like a mascot!"

I rolled my eyes, got out of the car, and hurried to Sylvie's front door. I didn't have to knock. The door swung open and I saw Sylvie.

"Oh my heck!" I yelled. "I love your hair!"

Sylvie was wearing a yellow headband that looked very cute.

"Thanks!" Sylvie said. "It keeps my bangs off my forehead."

"Nice," I said. Because I hadn't even thought of trying to keep my bangs off my forehead. Then I stepped into Sylvie's house and I saw something that I didn't want to see. I saw Malory, and she was wearing a headband too. Malory waved at me. I waved back with my fingers only, because my hands were full.

"What's in the box?" Malory asked.

"Tarts," I said.

"I love tarts!" Malory said.

Then Mrs. Potaski rounded the corner. My heart felt

jumpy. Even though we had made up at the window of the craft store, it still felt a little awkward standing face to face with her.

"Hi, Mrs. Potaski." I gave her a fingers-only wave too.

"Let me take those from you," Mrs. Potaski said. She reached down and took the box, but I kept my fur pants. Then she gave me a little hug. And it felt pretty terrific.

"Those are my bear pants," I said. "I'm a mascot."

Mrs. Potaski smiled at me. "I heard. And you jump rope."

I nodded.

"And you brought us tarts?" she asked.

"Yes," I said. "Blueberry. We each get our own."

"Lovely," Mrs. Potaski said. "Why don't you girls go catch up. I'll call you when lunch is ready."

"Cool," I said. Even though I only wanted to catch up with Sylvie.

"Let's go watch Taco!" Sylvie said.

Mrs. Potaski frowned a little. "If you take the ferret out of the cage, make sure your bedroom door is shut so he can't rampage through the house again."

"I know," Sylvie said.

"Malory's ferret rampaged through the house?" I asked. Because I was starting to like the ferret a little.

"Ferrets are pretty high-strung animals," Malory said. "Containment isn't in their nature."

"Oh," I said. That made sense.

When we got to Sylvie's bedroom, I spotted the ferret right away, because he was skinny and brown and chewing a hole in Sylvie's clothes hamper.

"Stop that, Taco!" Malory said.

But Taco didn't stop.

Malory scooped him up and held him to her chest. "Do you want to hold him? He loves sniffing new people."

I held my hands up. "Ferrets freak me out."

"Don't freak out," Sylvie said. She reached out and took hold of Taco. "This ferret is amazing. He knows geography."

I wasn't all that excited about walking into Sylvie's bedroom and meeting a ferret that knew geography. I wanted to learn bear dance moves. It was the whole reason I'd brought my fur pants.

"When are you going to teach me dance stuff?" I asked.

"After we play with Taco!" Sylvie said.

I decided I would play with Taco for ten minutes and then demand to learn dance moves.

"Taco can find any state on a map," Sylvie said.

But I didn't think that was all that special. Because I learned how to do that in third grade.

Sylvie pointed to a map of the United States that was spread out on her bedroom floor. Each state had a Cheerio on it. "Watch!" Sylvie said.

"Kentucky!" Malory said.

Sylvie set the ferret down and it lowered its nose to the map. It sniffed quickly, twitching its nose over and over.

"Does Kentucky smell different than other states?" I asked.

"Watch!" Sylvie said.

And then I watched as Taco walked across Texas and Louisiana. For a second it looked like he was going to turn south and go to Florida, but he didn't. He hurried up to Kentucky and ate the Cheerio.

"Wow," I said. "Your ferret knows Kentucky."

"Taco knows all the states," Malory said. "Vermont!"

I watched Taco scurry across the map, dislodging Cheerios from West Virginia, Pennsylvania, and New York as he hightailed it to Vermont.

It was impressive. "That ferret could be on TV," I said.

"I know," Malory said. She pulled at her headband and readjusted it. "First I want to teach him all the countries in Africa. Because I think my ferret has global potential."

"He does!" Sylvie said. Then she giggled and rushed toward Taco and plucked him off the map.

"I didn't know you liked ferrets so much," I said. Because as far as I knew, Taco was the first ferret Sylvie had ever seen.

Sylvie looked up at me and smiled. "I have learned so much about myself since school started."

"Oh," I said. I guess I'd learned some stuff about myself too. For instance, according to Principal Tidge, I had great comedic timing.

"Being brand-new is awesome," Sylvie said. She set Taco down on the carpet and he scampered to my feet. He sniffed my shoes and looked up at me.

"Does he bite?" I asked.

"It depends," Malory said.

I picked him up anyway, and he tried to burrow his head in my armpit, which I thought was pretty rude. But I guessed a ferret wouldn't know that.

It felt really weird to be standing in Sylvie's bedroom holding a ferret and not knowing what to say. So I sat down on Sylvie's bed. I liked being brand-new too. But I also missed things about my old life. Like Sylvie. And Grandma. And I didn't want to hide this from Sylvie.

"Being brand-new is harder than I thought," I said. "I mean, there's stuff I miss." When I said this, I looked directly at Sylvie.

Then Sylvie came and sat down next to me. When Taco tried to burrow his head in my armpit again, I put him on the floor.

"I know," Sylvie said. "I understand."

That meant a lot to me. Then I felt Sylvie hug me and that meant a lot to me too.

"I'm glad you're here hanging out with us," Sylvie said.

"Yeah," Malory said. "Sylvie is always telling funny stories about you."

"Really?" I asked.

I liked the idea of Sylvie always talking about me. Because it meant she was always thinking about me.

"Are you ready to learn some dance moves?" Sylvie asked.

I nodded.

"Ohh!" Malory said. "Have you ever done the robot? My brother taught me that one."

Sylvie and I glanced at each other and laughed. We hated the robot!

"What?" Malory asked, looking confused.

"No robot," Sylvie said.

"I agree," I said.

"I know! How about I teach you how to do the shimmy hips!" Sylvie said.

Then Sylvie hopped up on her bed and shook her hips back and forth, back and forth. She got them going so fast I thought her pants might fall down.

"Holy crud!" I said. "That looks cool. I need to put on my fur pants."

I slid on my pants and snapped the suspenders into place. Then I hopped up onto Sylvie's bed and so did Malory. We both started shaking our hips back and forth, back and forth. Malory did it while holding her ferret.

"You guys look great!" Sylvie said.

And I sort of agreed.

"Those fur pants look awesome!" Malory said.

Sylvie and Malory started laughing so hard when they watched me that they had to stop shimmying. But I didn't. I shimmied faster.

"I think it's the coolest thing you've ever done," Sylvie said. "You do it like a pro!"

But I couldn't thank her. Because I was pretty breathless. I flashed her a thumbs-up sign instead.

Back and forth. Back and forth. Back and forth.

"I want to come watch you do this at a game!" Sylvie said.

"Me too!" Malory said.

I finally stopped shimmying because it felt like I was going to die. Also, I needed to say something.

"I'd like that," I said while puffing a little. Because I couldn't think of anything better than shaking my butt like a wild animal or shimmying my hips like a pro in front of my friends.

"Do you want me to teach you the samba?" Sylvie asked. "You've definitely got the hips for it."

I smiled.

"What about krumping?" Malory asked. "She'd be great at the stomps and the wobbles."

I smiled wider.

"Lunch is ready!" Mrs. Potaski called.

I unsnapped my suspenders and slid off my fur pants. "I have an idea," I said. "After we eat our sandwiches and tarts, let's try both."

**KRISTEN TRACY** grew up in a small town in Idaho, where she learned a lot about bears. Sadly, she was not clever enough to reinvent herself in middle school. Also, technically, Kristen Tracy never went to middle school. She attended North Bonneville Junior High, where she took classes in industrial exploration (which involved lots of saws), Idaho history, public speaking, and keyboarding. Her least favorite class was PE, in which she was forced to run, tumble, hurdle, play shuffleboard, and perform the flexed-arm hang.

kristentracy.com